MY BOOK OF FAVORITE FAIRY TALES

MY BOOK OF
FAVORITE FAIRY TALES

Illustrated by Jennie Harbour

Derrydale Books
New York • Avenel, New Jersey

This edition
Copyright © 1993 by Outlet Book Company, Inc.

All rights reserved. First published in 1993 by Derrydale Books, distributed by Outlet Book Company, Inc., a Random House Company, 40 Engelhard Avenue, Avenel, New Jersey 07001

Random House
New York • Toronto • London • Sydney • Auckland
Designed by Eileen Rosenthal
Printed and bound in Singapore

Library of Congress Cataloging-in-Publication Data
My book of favorite fairy tales / illustrated by Jennie Harbour. p.   cm.
Summary: An illustrated collection of popular fairy tales, including "Hansel and Gretel," "Snow White," and "Beauty and the Beast."
ISBN 0-517-09125-9 : $8.99 1. Fairy tales.
[1. Fairy tales. 2. Folklore.] I. Harbour, Jennie, ill.
PZ8.M9855   1993   [398.2]—dc20   92-37669   CIP   AC

8   7   6   5   4   3   2   1

Contents

Introduction

HERE IS A WONDERFUL collection of marvelous fairy tales. Although all these stories were written a long, long time ago, they are always new and always will be, because there are always new children to read them.

Some of these stories may already be among your favorites. There's Little Red Riding Hood, who had a scary adventure, and dear, sweet Cinderella, and the lovely Sleeping Beauty. You'll meet Hansel and Gretel, the brave brother and sister, and Snowdrop, who you may know already as Snow White.

In this book you'll make the acquaintance, perhaps for the first time, of Princess Goldenhair and the courageous young man named Charming, wicked Bluebeard, the two good, kind sisters Snow White and Rose Red, funny, wise Tufty Riquet, and the amazing White Cat who must surely be something other than what she appears.

In this beautiful book, which is richly illustrated by Jennie Harbour, you'll be transported to a world of witches, fairies, and goblins. It is a magical world of blessings and curses, wonder and enchantment that has delighted many, many generations of children as they read their favorite fairy tales.

MY BOOK OF
FAVORITE
FAIRY TALES

Snowdrop

Once upon a time, in the middle of winter when the snowflakes were falling like feathers on the earth, a queen sat at a window framed in black ebony, and sewed. And as she sewed and gazed out at the white landscape, she pricked her finger with the needle, and three drops of blood fell on the snow outside, and because the red showed out so well against the white she thought to herself, Oh! what wouldn't I give to have a child as white as snow, as red as blood, and as black as ebony!

And her wish was granted, for not long after a little daughter was born to her, with skin as white as snow, lips and cheeks as red as blood, and hair as black as ebony. They called her Snowdrop. Soon after her birth the queen died. After a year the king married again. His new wife was a beautiful woman, but so proud and overbearing that she could not stand any rival to her beauty. She possessed a magic mirror, and when she used to stand before it gazing at her own reflection, and asked:

"Mirror, mirror, hanging there,
Who in all the land's most fair?"

it always replied:

"You are most fair, my Lady Queen.
None fairer in the land, I ween."

Then she was quite happy, for she knew the mirror always spoke the truth.

But Snowdrop was growing prettier and prettier every day, and when she was seven years old she was as beautiful as she could be, and fairer even than the queen herself.

One day when the queen asked her mirror the usual question, it replied:

"My Lady Queen, you are fair, 'tis true,
But Snowdrop is fairer far than you."

Then the queen flew into the most awful passion, and turned every shade of green in her jealousy. From this hour she hated poor Snowdrop, and every day her envy, hatred, and malice grew. At last she could endure Snowdrop's presence no longer, and, calling a huntsman to her, she said, "Take the child into the wood, and never let me see her face again. You must kill her, and bring me back proof that she is dead."

The huntsman did as he was told and led Snowdrop out into the wood, but as he was in the act of drawing out his knife to slay her, she began to cry, and said, "Oh, dear huntsman, spare my life, and I will promise to fly forth into the wide wood and never to return home again."

And because she was so young and pretty the huntsman had pity on her, and said, "Well, run along, poor child." For he thought to himself, The wild beasts will soon eat her up. And his heart felt lighter because he hadn't had to do the deed himself.

Now when the poor child found herself alone in the big wood the very

trees around her seemed to assume strange shapes, and she felt so frightened that she didn't know what to do. Then she began to run over the sharp stones, and through the bramble bushes, and the wild beasts ran past her, but they did her no harm.

She ran as far as her legs would carry her, and as evening approached she saw a little house, and she stepped inside to rest. Everything was very small in the little house, but cleaner and neater than anything you can imagine. In the middle of the room there stood a table, covered with a white tablecloth, and seven little plates and forks and spoons and knives and tumblers. Side by side against the wall there were seven little beds, covered with snow-white counterpanes.

Snowdrop felt so hungry and so thirsty that she ate a bit of bread and a little porridge from each plate, and drank a drop of wine out of each tumbler. Then, feeling tired and sleepy, she lay down on one of the beds, but it wasn't comfortable. Then she tried all the others in turn, but one was too long, and another too short, and it was only when she got to the seventh that she found one to suit her exactly. So she lay down upon it, said her prayers like a good child, and fell fast asleep.

When it got quite dark the masters of the little house returned. They

were seven dwarfs who worked in the mines right down deep in the heart of the mountain. They lighted their seven little lamps, and as soon as their eyes got accustomed to the glare they saw that someone had been in the room, for all was not in the same order as they had left it.

The first one said, "Who's been sitting in my chair?"

The second said, "Who's been eating my little loaf?"

The third said, "Who's been tasting my porridge?"

The fourth said, "Who's been eating out of my little plate?"

The fifth said, "Who's been using my little fork?"

The sixth said, "Who's been cutting with my little knife?"

The seventh said, "Who's been drinking out of my little tumbler?"

Then the first dwarf looked round and saw a little hollow in his bed, and he asked again, "Who's been lying on my bed?"

The others came running round, and cried when they saw their beds, "Somebody has lain on ours, too."

But when the seventh dwarf came to his bed he started back in amazement, for there he beheld Snowdrop fast asleep. Then he called to the others, who turned their little lamps full on the bed. When they saw Snowdrop lying there they nearly fell down with surprise.

"Goodness gracious!" they cried. "What a beautiful child!"

And they were so enchanted by her beauty that they did not wake her, but let her sleep on in the little bed. But the seventh dwarf slept with his companions one hour in each bed, and in this way he passed the night.

In the morning Snowdrop awoke, but when she saw the seven little dwarfs she felt very frightened. But they were so friendly, and asked her what her name was in such a kind way that she replied, "I am Snowdrop."

"Why did you come to our house?" continued the dwarfs.

Then she told them how her stepmother had wished her put to death, and how the huntsman had spared her life, and how she had run the whole day long till she had come to their little house.

The dwarfs, when they had heard her sad story, asked her, "Will you stay and keep house for us, cook, make the beds, do the washing, sew and knit? And if you give satisfaction and keep everything neat and clean, you shall want for nothing."

"Yes," answered Snowdrop, "I will gladly do all you ask."

And so she lived with them. Every morning the dwarfs went into the mountain, to dig for gold, and in the evening when they returned home, Snowdrop always had their supper ready for them. But during the day

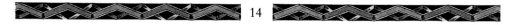

the girl was left quite alone, so the good dwarfs warned her, saying, "Beware of your stepmother. She will soon find out you are here, and whatever you do don't let anyone into the house."

Now the queen, supposing Snowdrop to be dead, never dreamed but that she was once more the most beautiful woman in the world; so stepping before her mirror one day she said:

"Mirror, mirror, hanging there,
Who in all the land's most fair?"

And the mirror replied:

"My Lady Queen, you are fair, 'tis true,
But Snowdrop is fairer far than you.
Snowdrop, who dwells with the seven little men,
Is as fair as you, as fair again."

When the queen heard these words she was nearly struck dumb with horror, for the mirror always spoke the truth, and she knew now that the huntsman must have deceived her, and that Snowdrop was still alive. She pondered day and night how she might destroy her, for as long as she felt she had a rival in the land her jealous heart left her no rest.

At last she hit upon a plan. She stained her face and dressed herself up as an old peddler wife, so that she was quite unrecognizable. In this guise she went over the seven hills until she came to the house of the seven dwarfs. Then she knocked at the door, calling out at the same time, "Fine wares to sell! Fine wares to sell!"

Snowdrop peeped out of the window, and called out, "Good day, mother. What have you to sell?"

"Good wares, fine wares," she answered, "laces of every shade and description," and she held up one that was made of some gay-colored silk.

Surely I can let the honest woman in, thought Snowdrop; so she unbarred the door and bought the pretty lace.

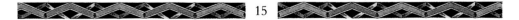

"Good gracious, child!" said the old woman, "what a figure you've got! Come, I'll lace you up properly for once."

Snowdrop, suspecting no evil, stood before her and let her lace her bodice up, but the old woman laced her so quickly and so tightly that it took Snowdrop's breath away, and she fell down dead.

"Now you are no longer the fairest," said the wicked old woman, and then she hastened away.

In the evening the seven dwarfs came home. What a fright they got when they saw their dead Snowdrop lying on the floor, as still and motionless as a dead person! They lifted her up tenderly and when they saw how tightly laced she was they cut the lace in two, and she began to breathe a little and gradually came back to life.

When the dwarfs heard what had happened they said, "Depend upon it, the old peddler wife was none other than the old queen. In the future you must be sure to let no one in, if we are not at home."

As soon as the wicked old queen got home she went straight to her mirror and said:

> "Mirror, mirror, hanging there,
> Who in all the land's most fair?"

and the mirror answered as before:

> "My Lady Queen, you are fair, 'tis true,
> But Snowdrop is fairer far than you.
> Snowdrop, who dwells with the seven little men,
> Is as fair as you, as fair again."

When she heard this she became as pale as death, because she saw at once that Snowdrop must be alive again.

"This time," she said to herself, "I will think of something that will make an end of her once and for all."

And using the witchcraft which she understood so well the queen made a poisonous comb. Then she dressed herself up and assumed the form of

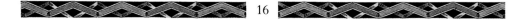

another old woman. So she went over the seven hills till she reached the house of the seven dwarfs, and knocking at the door she called out, "Fine wares for sale!"

Snowdrop looked out of the window and said, "You must go away, for I may not let anyone in."

"But surely you are not forbidden to look out?" said the old woman, and she held up the poisonous comb for her to see.

It pleased the girl so much that she let herself be taken in, and opened the door. When they had settled their bargain the old woman said, "Now I'll comb your hair properly for you."

Poor Snowdrop thought no evil, but hardly had the comb touched her hair than the poison worked and she fell down unconscious.

"Now, my fine lady, you're really done for this time," said the wicked woman, and she made her way home as fast as she could.

Fortunately, it was now near evening, and the seven dwarfs returned home. When they saw Snowdrop lying dead on the ground, they at once suspected that her wicked stepmother had been at work again. They searched till they found the poisonous comb, and the moment they pulled it out of her hair Snowdrop came to herself again, and told them what had happened. Then they warned her once more to be on her guard, and to open the door to no one.

As soon as the queen got home she went straight to her mirror, and asked:

"Mirror, mirror, hanging there,
Who in all the land's most fair?"

And it replied as before:

"My Lady Queen, you are fair, 'tis true,
But Snowdrop is fairer far than you.
Snowdrop, who dwells with the seven little men,
Is as fair as you, as fair again."

When the queen heard this she literally trembled and shook with rage. "Snowdrop shall die," she cried, "yes, though it cost me my own life." Then she went to the little secret chamber, which no one knew of but herself, and there she made a poisonous apple. Outwardly it looked beautiful, green with red cheeks, so that everyone who saw it longed to eat it, but anyone who might do so would certainly die on the spot. When the apple was quite finished she stained her face and dressed herself as a peasant, and so she went over the seven hills to the seven dwarfs. She knocked at the door, as usual, but Snowdrop put her head out of the window and called out, "I may not let anyone in. The seven dwarfs have forbidden me to do so."

"Are you afraid of being poisoned?" asked the old woman. "See, I will

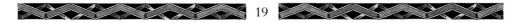

cut this apple in half. I'll eat the green cheek and you can eat the red."

But the apple was so cunningly made that only the red cheek was poisonous. Snowdrop longed to eat the tempting fruit, and when she saw the peasant woman was eating it herself, she couldn't resist the temptation any longer. Stretching out her hand she took the poisonous half. But hardly had the first bite passed her lips than she fell down dead on the ground. Then the eyes of the cruel queen sparkled with glee, and laughing aloud, she cried, "As white as snow, as red as blood, and as black as ebony, this time the dwarfs won't be able to bring you back to life."

When she got home she asked the mirror:

"Mirror, mirror, hanging there,
Who in all the land's most fair?"

And this time it replied:

"You are most fair, my Lady Queen,
None fairer in the land, I ween."

Then her jealous heart was at rest—at least as much at rest as a jealous heart can ever be.

When evening came, the dwarfs returned home. They found Snowdrop lying on the ground: no breath passed her lips, and they were afraid that she was quite dead. They lifted her up, and combed her hair, and washed her face with wine and water. But all was in vain, for the little girl seemed quite dead. So they laid her down upon a bier, and all seven watched and bewailed her for three whole days. Then they proposed to bury her, but her cheeks were still rosy, and her face looked just as it did while she was alive; so they said, "We will never bury her in the cold ground," and they made a coffin of glass so that they still might look at her, and wrote her name upon it in golden letters, and that she was a king's daughter.

The coffin was placed upon the hill, and one of the dwarfs always sat by it and watched. And the birds of the air came, too, and bemoaned

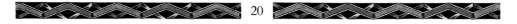

Snowdrop. First of all came an owl, and then a raven, but at last came a
dove.

And thus Snowdrop lay for a long, long time, and still only looked as
though she were asleep; for even now she was as white as snow, and as
red as blood, and as black as ebony.

At last a prince came and called at the dwarfs' house. He saw Snowdrop, and read what was written in gold letters. Then he offered the
dwarfs money, and earnestly prayed them to let him take her away. But
they said, "We will not part with her for all the gold in the world." At
last, however, they had pity on him, and gave him the coffin. But the
moment he lifted it up to carry it home with him, the piece of apple fell
from between her lips, and Snowdrop awoke and said, "Where am I?"

The prince answered, "Thou art safe with me." Then he told her all
that had happened, and said, "I love you better than all the world. Come
with me to my father's palace, and you shall be my wife."

And Snowdrop consented, and went home with the prince; and every-

thing was prepared with great pomp and splendor for their wedding.

To the feast was invited, among the rest, Snowdrop's old enemy, the queen. As she was dressing herself in fine rich clothes, she looked in the glass and said:

> "Tell me, mirror, tell me true!
> Of all the ladies in the land
> Who is fairest? tell me who?"

And the glass answered:

> "Thou, lady, are loveliest here, I ween;
> But lovelier far is the new-made queen."

When the queen heard this, she started with rage. But her envy and curiosity were so great that she could not help setting out to see the bride. And when she arrived, and saw that it was no other than Snowdrop, who, as she thought, had been dead a long while, she choked with passion, and fell ill and died. Snowdrop and the prince lived and reigned happily over that land for many, many years.

Cinderella

Once there was a gentleman who married for his second wife the proudest and most haughty woman that was ever seen. She had by a former husband two daughters who were exactly like her in all things. He had, by his first wife who had died, a young daughter who was good and sweet and very pretty.

No sooner was the wedding ceremony over but the new wife began to show herself in her true colors. She could not bear the good qualities of this pretty girl, perhaps because they made her own daughters appear the more odious. She employed her in the meanest work of the house. Her room was in the garret, and she slept upon a wretched straw bed, while her stepsisters had fine rooms, with floors all inlaid, beds of the very newest fashion, and looking-glasses so large that they could see themselves at their full length from head to foot.

The poor girl bore it all patiently. She dared not tell her father, who

would not have believed her, for his new wife governed him entirely.
When she had done her work she used to go into the chimney corner and
sit down among the cinders and ashes. The youngest daughter, who was
not so rude and uncivil as the eldest, called her Cinderella. However,
Cinderella, notwithstanding the ragged clothes she was given to wear,

was a hundred times handsomer than her sisters, although they were always richly dressed.

It happened that the king's son was to give a ball and he invited all persons of fashion to it. The young stepsisters were among those invited. They were delighted at the invitation, and wonderfully busy in choosing the gowns, petticoats, and jewelry as might become them. This created even more work for Cinderella, for it was she who ironed her sisters' linen and pleated their ruffles. They talked all day long of nothing but how they should be dressed.

"For my part," said the eldest, "I will wear a red velvet gown with French trimming."

"And I," said the youngest, "shall have my usual petticoat. But then, to make amends for that, I will put on my gold-flowered manteau and my diamond necklace."

Cinderella was called up to be consulted in all these matters, for she had excellent taste and advised them always for the best. She also offered to do their hair, which they were very willing she should do. As she was doing this they said to her, "Cinderella, would you not like to go to the ball?"

"Alas!" said she, "you make fun of me. It is not for such as I am to go to the prince's ball."

"You are right about that," replied the elder sister. "It would make the people laugh to see a cinder wench at a ball."

When they were finally dressed and left for the palace, Cinderella sat in the chimney corner and began to cry.

Her godmother, who saw her all in tears, asked her what was the matter.

"I wish I could—I wish I could—"

She was not able to speak the rest, being interrupted by her sobbing.

This godmother of hers, who was a fairy, said to her, "Thou wishest thou couldst go to the ball. Is it not so?"

"Yes," cried Cinderella, with a great sigh.

"Well," said her godmother, "be a good girl, and I will contrive that thou shalt go." Then she took her into her chamber and said to her, "Run into the garden and bring me a pumpkin."

Cinderella went immediately to gather the finest she could get, and brought it to her godmother, not being able to imagine how this pumpkin could make her go to the ball. Her godmother scooped out the inside of it, leaving nothing but the rind. This done, she struck it with her wand, and the pumpkin was instantly turned into a fine coach, gilded all over with gold.

She then went to look into her mousetrap, where she found six mice, all alive. She ordered Cinderella to lift up the trapdoor a little. Then, giving each mouse as it went out a little tap with her wand, the mouse instantly turned into a fine horse, This made a fine set of six horses of a beautiful mouse-colored dapple-gray. Being at a loss for a coachman, Cinderella said, "I will go and see if there is a rat in the rat trap. We could make a coachman of him."

"Thou art quite right," replied her godmother. "Go and look."

Cinderella brought the trap to her, and in it there were three huge rats. The fairy chose the one which had the largest beard, and having touched him with her wand he was turned into a fat, jolly coachman with fine whiskers. After that she said to Cinderella: "Go again into the garden, and you will find six lizards behind the watering pot. Bring them to me."

Cinderella had no sooner done so but her godmother turned them into six footmen, who skipped up immediately behind the coach, with their liveries all bedaubed with gold and silver, and clung as close behind each other as if they had done nothing else their whole lives.

The fairy then said to Cinderella, "Well, thou see here an equipage fit to go to the ball with. Art thou not pleased with it?"

"Oh! yes," she cried, "but must I go there as I am, in these nasty rags?"

Her godmother only just touched her with her wand, and at the same instant her clothes were turned into cloth-of-gold and silver, all beset with jewels. This done, she gave her a pair of glass slippers, the prettiest in the whole world. Then Cinderella got into her coach. Before she left her godmother commanded her not to stay until after midnight. "If you stay one moment longer," she said, "the coach will be a pumpkin again, the horses mice, the coachman a rat, the footmen lizards, and your clothes will become just as they were before."

Cinderella promised her godmother she would not fail to leave the ball before midnight. And then away she drove, hardly able to contain herself for joy.

The king's son, who was told that a great princess, whom nobody knew, had arrived, ran out to receive her. He gave her his hand as she alighted from the coach, and led her into the hall among all the guests. There was immediately a profound silence, they stopped dancing, and the violins ceased to play, so stunned was everyone by the great beauty of the unknown newcomer. Then, nothing was heard but a confused noise of "Ah! how lovely she is! Ah! how lovely she is!"

The king himself, old as he was, could not help watching her and telling the queen softly that it was a long time since he had seen so beautiful and lovely a creature.

All the ladies studied her gown, that they might have one made after the same pattern—provided they could find such fine materials and able hands to make it.

The king's son conducted Cinderella to the seat of honor and afterward asked her to dance with him. She danced so very gracefully that everyone admired her more and more. A fine meal was served, but the young prince ate not a morsel, so intent was he with gazing at her.

Cinderella went and sat down next to her stepsisters. She was very kind to them, giving them some of the choicest tidbits which the prince had presented to her. This very much surprised them, for they did not recognize her. While Cinderella was thus amusing her sisters, she heard the clock strike eleven and three-quarters. She immediately made a courtesy to the king and queen and hastened away as fast as she could.

On arriving home, she ran to find her godmother. After thanking her she said she could not but wish she might go the next day to another ball, to which the king's son had invited her.

As she was eagerly telling her godmother everything that had happened at the ball her two sisters knocked at the door. Cinderella ran and opened.

"How long you stayed!" she cried, rubbing her eyes, and stretching as if she had just been waked out of her sleep.

"If you had been at the ball," said one of her sisters, "you would not have been tired with it. There came there the finest princess, the most beautiful ever seen with mortal eyes. She was very kind to us and even gave us some tidbits."

Cinderella seemed very indifferent. She asked them the name of that princess, but they told her they did not know it, and that the king's son

would give all the world to know who she was. At this Cinderella, smiling, replied, "She must, then, be very beautiful indeed."

The next day the two sisters went to the ball, and so did Cinderella, who was dressed more magnificently than before. The king's son was always near her and never ceased his compliments and kind speeches to her. Cinderella was enjoying herself so much that she quite forgot what her godmother had told to her, so that she at last counted the clock striking twelve when she took it to be no more than eleven.

She rose and fled as nimble as a deer. The prince followed, but could not overtake her. In her hurry she dropped one of her glass slippers, which the prince picked up most carefully. Cinderella arrived home, quite out of breath and in her old clothes, having nothing left her of all her finery but the other one of the little slippers. When the prince asked the guards at the palace gate if they had not seen a princess leave they replied that they had seen nobody go out but a young girl, dressed in rags.

When the two sisters returned from the ball, Cinderella asked them if they had enjoyed themselves and if the fine lady had been there.

They told her yes, but that she hurried away as soon as the clock struck twelve, and with so much haste that she dropped one of her little glass slippers, the prettiest in the world, which the king's son had found. They said that the prince had done nothing but look at her at the ball and that most certainly he was very much in love with the beautiful person who owned the glass slipper.

What they said was very true, for a few days later the king's son had it proclaimed, by sound of trumpet, that he would marry her whose foot this slipper would just fit. His courtiers were sent to try the slipper first upon the princesses, then the duchesses, and then all the ladies of the court. But in vain. Finally, the slipper was brought to the two sisters. Each did all she possibly could to thrust her foot into the slipper. But it fit neither.

Cinderella, who was watching, said to them, laughing, "Let me see if it will not fit me."

Her sisters burst out laughing. But the gentleman who was sent to try the slipper looked earnestly at Cinderella, and seeing that she was very lovely despite her ragged clothes said it was only fair that she should try, and that he had orders to let everyone make trial.

He asked Cinderella to sit down, and putting the slipper to her foot he found it went on very easily and fit her as if it had been made of wax. Her two sisters' astonishment was excessively great, but still abundantly greater when Cinderella pulled out of her pocket the other slipper and put it on her foot. Thereupon in came her godmother, who touched Cinderella's clothes with her wand, and made them richer and more magnificent than any she had worn before.

And now when her two sisters saw her to be that fine, beautiful lady who was at the ball, they threw themselves at her feet to beg pardon for all their ill-treatment of her. Cinderella embraced them and cried that she forgave them with all her heart and desired them always to love her.

She was then conducted to the young prince. He thought her more charming than ever and a few days later they were married. Cinderella, who was no less good than beautiful, gave her two sisters lodgings in the palace, and that very same day matched them with two lords of the court.

Princess Goldenhair

Once upon a time there was a princess who was the prettiest creature in the world. And because she was so beautiful, and because her hair was like the finest gold and waved and rippled nearly to the ground, she was called the Princess Goldenhair. She always wore a crown of flowers, and her dresses were embroidered with diamonds and pearls, and everybody who saw her fell in love with her.

Now, one of her neighbors was a young king who was not married. He was very rich and handsome, and when he heard all that was said about the Princess Goldenhair, though he had never seen her, he fell so deeply in love with her that he could neither eat nor drink. So he resolved to send an ambassador to ask her hand in marriage. He had a splendid carriage made for his ambassador, and gave him more than a hundred horses and a hundred servants, and told him to be sure to bring the princess back with him.

After the ambassador left on his mission, nothing else was talked of at

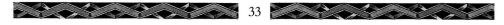

court. The king felt so sure that the princess would consent that he set his people to work making pretty dresses and splendid furniture, that they might be ready by the time she came.

Meanwhile the ambassador arrived at the princess's palace and delivered his message, but whether she happened to be cross that day, or whether the compliment did not please her, is not known. She only answered that she was very much obliged to the king, but she had no wish to be married.

The ambassador set off sadly on his homeward way, bringing all the king's presents back with him, for the princess was too well brought up to accept the pearls and diamonds when she would not accept the king. She had only kept twenty-five English pins that he might not be vexed.

When the ambassador reached the city, where the king was waiting impatiently, everybody was very much annoyed with him for not bringing the princess. The king cried like a baby, and nobody could console him.

Now, there was at the court a young man, who was more clever and handsome than anyone else. He was called Charming, and everyone loved him, excepting a few envious people who were angry at his being the king's favorite and knowing all the state secrets. One day he happened to be with some people who were speaking of the ambassador's return and saying that his going to the princess had not done much good, when Charming said rashly, "If the king had sent me to the Princess Goldenhair I am sure she would have come back with me."

His enemies at once went to the king and said, "You will hardly believe, sire, what Charming has the audacity to say—that if he had been sent to the Princess Goldenhair she would certainly have come back with him. He seems to think that he is so much handsomer than you that the princess would have fallen in love with him and followed him willingly." The king was very angry when he heard this.

"Ha! ha!" said he. "Does he laugh at my unhappiness and think himself more fascinating than I am? Let him be shut up in my great tower to die of hunger."

So the king's guards went to fetch Charming, who had thought no more of his rash speech, and carried him off to prison with great cruelty. The poor prisoner had only a little straw for his bed, and were it not for a little stream of water which flowed through the tower he would have died of thirst.

One day when he was in despair he said to himself, "How can I have offended the king? I am his most faithful subject and have done nothing against him."

The king chanced to be passing the tower and recognized the voice of his former favorite. He stopped to listen in spite of Charming's enemies, who tried to persuade him to have nothing more to do with the traitor. But the king said, "Be quiet. I wish to hear what he says."

And then he opened the tower door and called to Charming, who came

very sadly and kissed the king's hand, saying, "What have I done, sire, to deserve this cruel treatment?"

"You mocked me and my ambassador," said the king, "and you said that if I had sent you for the Princess Goldenhair you would certainly have brought her back."

"It is quite true, sire," replied Charming. "I should have drawn such a picture of you, and represented your good qualities in such a way that I am certain the princess would have found you irresistible. But I cannot see what there is in that to make you angry."

The king could not see any cause for anger either when the matter was presented to him in this light, and he began to frown very fiercely at the courtiers who had so misrepresented his favorite.

So he took Charming back to the palace with him, and after seeing that he had a very good supper he said to him, "You know that I love the Princess Goldenhair as much as ever. Her refusal has not made any difference to me. But I don't know how to make her change her mind. I really should like to send you, to see if you can persuade her to marry me."

Charming replied that he was perfectly willing to go, and would set out the very next day.

"But you must wait until I can get a grand escort for you," said the king. But Charming said that he only wanted a good horse to ride, and the king, who was delighted at his being ready to start so promptly, gave him letters to the princess and bade him good speed.

It was on a Monday morning that Charming set out all alone upon his errand, thinking of nothing but how he could persuade the Princess Goldenhair to marry the king. He had a writing book in his pocket, and

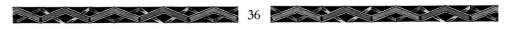

whenever any happy thought struck him he dismounted from his horse and sat down under the trees to put it into the argument, which he was preparing for the princess, before he forgot it.

One day when he had started at the very earliest dawn and was riding over a great meadow, he suddenly had a marvelous idea. Springing from his horse, he sat down under a willow tree which grew by a little river. When he had written it down he was looking around him, pleased to find himself in such a pretty place, when he saw a great golden carp lying gasping and exhausted upon the grass. In leaping after little flies she had thrown herself high upon the bank, where she had lain until she was nearly dead. Charming had pity upon the carp, and though he couldn't help thinking that she would have been very nice for dinner, he picked her up gently and put her back into the water.

As soon as Dame Carp felt the refreshing coolness of the water she sank down joyfully to the bottom of the river. Then swimming up to the bank quite boldly she said, "I thank you, Charming, for the kindness you have done me. You have saved my life. One day I will repay you." So saying, she sank down into the water again, leaving Charming greatly astonished at her politeness.

Another day, as he journeyed on, he saw a raven in great distress. The poor bird was closely pursued by an eagle, which would soon have eaten it had not Charming quickly fitted an arrow to his bow and shot the eagle dead. The raven perched upon a tree very joyfully.

"Charming," said he, "it was very generous of you to rescue a poor raven. I am not ungrateful and some day I will repay you."

Charming thought it was very nice of the raven to say so, and went on his way.

Before the sun rose he found himself in a thick wood, where it was too dark for him to see his path. Here he heard an owl crying as if it were in despair.

"Hark!" said he, "that sounds like an owl in great trouble. I am sure it has got into a snare." And he began to hunt about. Presently he found a

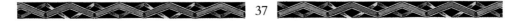

great net which some birdcatchers must have spread the night before.

"What a pity it is that men do nothing but torment and persecute poor creatures which never do them any harm!" said he, and he took out his knife and cut the net. The owl flitted away into the darkness, but then turning, with one flicker of her wings, she came back to Charming and said, "It does not need many words to tell you how great a service you have done me. I was caught. In a few minutes the fowlers would have been here. Without your help I should have been killed. I am grateful, and one day I will repay you."

These three adventures were the only ones of any consequence that befell Charming upon his journey, and he made all the haste he could to reach the palace of the Princess Goldenhair.

When he arrived he thought everything he saw delightful and magnif-icent. Diamonds were as plentiful as pebbles and the gold and silver, the beautiful dresses, the sweetmeats and pretty things that were everywhere quite amazed him. He thought to himself, If the princess consents to leave all this and come with me to marry the king, he may think himself lucky!

Then he dressed himself carefully in rich brocade, with scarlet and white plumes, and threw a splendid embroidered scarf over his shoulder. Looking as gay and as graceful as possible, he presented himself at the door of the palace, carrying in his arm a tiny pretty dog which he had bought on the way. The guards saluted him respectfully, and a messenger was sent to the princess to announce the arrival of Charming as ambas-sador of her neighbor the king.

" 'Charming,' " said the princess. "The name promises well. I have no doubt that he is good-looking and fascinates everybody."

"Indeed he does, madam," said all her maids of honor in one breath. "We saw him from the window of the garret where we were spinning flax, and we could do nothing but look at him as long as he was in sight."

"Well, to be sure!" said the princess. "That's how you amuse your-selves, is it? Looking at strangers out of the window! Be quick and give me my blue satin embroidered dress, and comb out my golden hair. Let somebody make me fresh garlands of flowers, and give me my high-heeled shoes and my fan, and tell them to sweep my great hall and my throne."

All her maids scurried this way and that to make the princess ready, and in their haste they knocked their heads together and hindered each other, until she thought they would never be finished. However, at last they led her into the gallery of mirrors, that she might assure herself that nothing was lacking in her appearance. Then she mounted her throne of gold, ebony, and ivory, while her ladies took their guitars and began to sing softly. Charming was led in, and was so struck with astonishment and admiration that at first not a word could he say. But presently he took courage and delivered his argument, bravely ending by begging the princess to spare him the disappointment of going back without her.

"Sir Charming," answered she, "all the reasons you have given me are very good ones. I assure you that I should have more pleasure in obliging you than anyone else, but you must know that a month ago as I was walking by the river with my ladies I took off my glove, and as I did so a ring that I was wearing slipped off my finger and rolled into the water. As I valued it more than my kingdom, you may imagine how vexed I was at losing it. I vowed never to listen to any proposal of marriage unless the ambassador first brought me back my ring. So now you know what is expected of you, for if you talked for fifteen days and fifteen nights you could not make me change my mind."

Charming was very surprised by this answer, but he bowed low to the princess and begged her to accept the embroidered scarf and the tiny dog he had brought with him. But she answered that she did not want any presents, and that he was to remember what she had just told him.

When Charming got back to his lodging he went to bed without eating any supper, and his little dog, who was called Frisk, couldn't eat any either, but came and lay down close to him. All night long Charming sighed and lamented.

"How am I to find a ring that fell into the river a month ago?" said he. "It is useless to try. The princess must have told me to do it on purpose, knowing it was impossible." And then he sighed again.

Frisk heard him and said, "My dear master, don't despair; the luck may change. You are too good not to be happy. Let us go down to the river as soon as it is light."

But Charming only gave him two little pats and said nothing, and soon he fell asleep.

At the first glimmer of dawn, Frisk began to jump about. When he had waked Charming they went out together, first into the garden, and then down to the river's edge, where they wandered up and down. Charming was thinking sadly of having to go back unsuccessful, when he heard someone calling, "Charming! Charming!" He looked all about him and thought he must be dreaming, as he could not see anybody. Then he walked on and the voice called again, "Charming! Charming!"

"Who calls me?" said he.

Frisk, who was very small and could look closely into the water, cried out, "I see a golden carp coming."

And sure enough there was the great carp, who said to Charming, "You saved my life in the meadow by the willow tree, and I promised that I would repay you. Take this. It is the Princess Goldenhair's ring."

Charming took the ring out of Dame Carp's mouth, thanking her a thousand times, and he and tiny Frisk went straight to the palace, where someone told the princess that he was asking to see her.

"Ah! poor fellow," said she, "he must have come to say goodbye, finding it impossible to do as I asked."

In came Charming, who presented her with the ring and said, "Madam, I have done your bidding. Will it please you to marry my master?" When the princess saw her ring brought back to her unhurt she was so astonished that she thought she must be dreaming.

"Truly, Charming," said she, "you must be the favorite of some fairy, or you could never have found it."

"Madam," he answered, "I was helped by nothing but my desire to obey your wishes."

"Since you are so kind," she said, "perhaps you will do me another service, for until it is done I will never be married. There is a prince not far from here whose name is Galifron. He once wanted to marry me, but when I refused he uttered the most terrible threats against me, and vowed that he would lay waste my country. But what could I do? I could not marry a frightful giant as tall as a tower, who eats people as a monkey eats chestnuts, and who talks so loud that anybody who has to listen to him becomes quite deaf. Nevertheless, he does not cease to persecute me and to kill my subjects. So before I can listen to your proposal you must kill him and bring me his head."

Charming was rather dismayed at this command, but he answered,

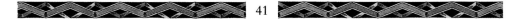

"Very well, princess, I will fight this Galifron. I believe that he will kill me, but at any rate I shall die in your defense."

The princess was frightened and said everything she could think of to prevent Charming from fighting the giant, but it was of no use. He went out to arm himself suitably, and then, taking little Frisk with him, he mounted his horse and set out for Galifron's country.

Everyone he met told him what a terrible giant Galifron was, and that nobody dared go near him. The more he heard the more frightened he grew. Frisk tried to encourage him by saying, "While you are fighting the giant, dear master, I will go and bite his heels, and when he stoops down to look at me you can kill him."

Charming praised his little dog's plan, but he knew that his help would not do much good.

At last he drew near the giant's castle, and saw to his horror that every path that led to it was strewn with bones. Before long he saw Galifron coming. His head was higher than the tallest trees, and he sang in a terrible voice:

> "Bring out your little boys and girls,
>   Pray do not stay to do their curls,
>   For I shall eat so very many,
>   I shall not know if they have any."

Thereupon Charming sang out as loud as he could to the same tune:

> "Come out and meet the valiant Charming,
>   Who finds you not at all alarming;
>   Although he is not very tall,
>   He's big enough to make you fall."

The rhymes were not very correct, but he had made them up so quickly that it is a miracle that they were not worse; especially since he was horribly frightened all the time.

When Galifron heard these words he looked all about him, and saw

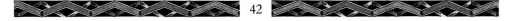

Charming standing, sword in hand. This put the giant into a terrible rage. He aimed a blow at Charming with his huge iron club which would certainly have killed him if it had reached him. But at that instant a raven perched upon the giant's head, and pecking with its strong beak and beating with its great wings, so confused and blinded him that all his blows fell harmlessly upon the air. Charming, rushing in, gave him several strokes with his sharp sword so that he fell to the ground. Whereupon Charming cut off his head before he knew anything about it.

The raven from a tree close by croaked out, "You see, I have not forgotten the good turn you did me in killing the eagle. Today I think I have fulfilled my promise of repaying you."

"Indeed, I owe you more gratitude than you ever owed me," replied Charming. And then he mounted his horse and rode off with Galifron's head.

When he reached the city the people ran after him in crowds, crying, "Behold the brave Charming, who has killed the giant!"

And their shouts reached the princess's ear, but she dared not ask what was happening, for fear she should hear that Charming had been killed. But very soon he arrived at the palace with the giant's head, of which she was still terrified, though it could no longer do her any harm.

"Princess," said Charming, "I have killed your enemy. I hope you will now consent to marry the king my master."

"Oh, dear! no," said the princess. "Not until you have brought me some water from the gloomy cavern. Not far from here there is a deep cave, the entrance to which is guarded by two dragons with fiery eyes, who will not allow anyone to pass them. When you get into the cavern you will find an immense hole, which you must go down. It is full of toads and snakes. At the bottom of this hole there is another little cave, in which rises the fountain of health and beauty. It is some of this water that I really must have. Everything it touches becomes wonderful. Beautiful things will always remain beautiful and ugly things become lovely. If one is young one never grows old, and if one is old one becomes young. You

see, Charming, I could not leave my kingdom without taking some of it with me."

"Princess," said he, "you certainly will never need this water, but I am an unhappy ambassador whose death you desire. Where you send me I will go, though I shall never return."

And as the Princess Goldenhair showed no sign of relenting, he started with his little dog for the gloomy cavern.

Everyone he met on the way said, "What a pity that a handsome young man should throw away his life so carelessly! He is going to the cavern alone, though if he had a hundred men with him he could not succeed. Why does the princess ask impossibilities?"

Charming said nothing, but he was very sad. When he was near the top of a hill he dismounted to let his horse graze, while Frisk amused himself by chasing flies. Charming knew he could not be far from the gloomy cavern. Looking about him he saw a black hideous rock from which came thick smoke, followed in a moment by one of the dragons with fire blazing from his mouth and eyes. His body was yellow and green and his claws were scarlet. His tail was so long that it lay in a hundred coils. Frisk was so terrified at the sight of it that he did not know where to hide.

Charming, quite determined to get the water or die, drew his sword,

and taking the crystal flask which Princess Goldenhair had given him to fill, said to Frisk, "I feel sure that I shall never come back from this expedition. When I am dead, go to the princess and tell her that her errand has cost me my life. Then find the king, my master, and relate all my adventures to him."

As he spoke he heard a voice calling, "Charming! Charming!"

"Who calls me?" said he. Then he saw an owl sitting in a hollow tree, who said to him, "You saved my life when I was caught in the net. Now I can repay you. Trust me with the flask, for I know all the ways of the gloomy cavern and can fill it from the fountain of beauty."

Charming was only too glad to give the owl the flask, and she flitted into the cavern quite unnoticed by the dragon. After some time she returned with the flask, filled to the very brim with sparking water. Charming thanked the owl with all his heart and joyfully hastened back to the town.

He went straight to the palace and gave the flask to the princess, who had no further objection to make. So she thanked Charming and ordered that preparations should be made for her departure.

The next day they set out together. The princess found Charming such an agreeable companion that she sometimes said to him, "Why didn't we stay where we were? I could have made you king and we should have been so happy!"

But Charming only answered, "I could not have done anything that would have vexed my master so much, even for a kingdom, or to please you, though I think you are as beautiful as the sun."

At last they reached the king's great city, and he came out to meet the princess, bringing magnificent presents, and the marriage was celebrated with great rejoicings. But Goldenhair was so fond of Charming that she could not be happy unless he was near her, and she was always singing his praises.

"If it hadn't been for Charming," she said to the king, "I should never have come here. You ought to be very much obliged to him, for he did the most impossible things and got me water from the fountain of beauty, so I can never grow old and shall get prettier every year."

Then Charming's enemies said to the king, "It is a wonder that you are not jealous. The queen thinks there is nobody in the world like Charming. As if anybody you had sent could not have done just as much!"

"It is quite true, now that I come to think of it," said the king. "Let him be chained hand and foot and thrown into the tower."

So they took Charming, and as a reward for having served the king so faithfully he was shut up in the tower, where he only saw the jailor, who brought him a piece of black bread and a pitcher of water every day.

Little Frisk came to console him, however, and told him all the news.

When Goldenhair heard what had happened she threw herself at the king's feet and begged him to set Charming free. But the more she cried the more angry he was, and at last she saw that it was useless to say any more. But it made her very sad. Then the king took it into his head that perhaps he was not handsome enough to please Queen Goldenhair. He thought he would bathe his face with the water from the fountain of beauty, which was in the flask on a shelf in the princess's room, where she had placed it that she might see it often. Now, it happened that one of the princess's ladies in chasing a spider had knocked the flask off the shelf and broken it. Every drop of the water had been spilled. Not knowing what to do, she had hastily swept away the pieces of crystal. She then remembered that in the king's room she had seen a flask of exactly the same shape, also filled with sparking water. So, without saying a word, she fetched it and stood it upon the queen's shelf.

Now, the water in this flask was what was used in the kingdom for getting rid of troublesome people. Instead of having their heads cut off in the usual way, their faces were bathed with the water, and they instantly fell asleep and never woke up again.

So when the king, thinking to improve his beauty, took the flask and sprinkled the water upon his face, he fell asleep. Nobody could wake him.

Little Frisk was the first to hear the news, and he ran to tell Charming,

who sent him to beg the princess not to forget the poor prisoner. All the palace was in confusion because of the king's death, but tiny Frisk made his way through the crowd to the princess's side and said, "Madam, do not forget poor Charming!"

Then she remembered all Charming had done for her. Without saying a word to anyone she went straight to the tower, and with her own hands took off Charming's chains. Then, putting a golden crown upon his head and the royal mantle upon his shoulders, she said, "Come, faithful Charming. I make you king and will take you for my husband."

Charming, once more free and happy, fell at her feet and thanked her for her gracious words.

Everybody was delighted that he should be king, and the wedding, which took place at once, was the prettiest that can be imagined, and Prince Charming and the Princess Goldenhair lived happily ever after.

Little Red Riding Hood

Many years ago there lived a dear little girl, who was beloved by everyone who knew her. But she was especially dear to her grandmother who never felt that she could think and do enough for her. On her granddaughter's birthday she presented her with a red velvet cloak with a hood. It suited her so well and she liked it so much that she would never wear anything else. And so she was called Little Red Riding Hood.

One day her mother said to her, "Come, Red Riding Hood, here is a nice piece of meat, and a bottle of wine. Take these to your grandmother. She is weak and ailing, and they will do her good. Be there before she gets up. Go quietly and carefully and do not run, or you may fall and break the bottle. When you go into your grandmother's room, do not forget to say 'Good morning' and do not pry into all the corners."

"I will do just as you say," answered Red Riding Hood, bidding good-bye to her mother.

The grandmother lived far away in the wood, a long walk from the village. When Little Red Riding Hood reached the wood she met a wolf. She did not know what a wicked animal it was, and so she was not at all frightened.

"Good morning, Little Red Riding Hood," he said.

"Thank you, Mr. Wolf," she said.

"Where are you going so early, Little Red Riding Hood?"

"To my grandmother's," she answered.

"And what are you carrying under your apron?"

"Some wine and meat," she replied. "We baked the meat yesterday, so that grandmother, who is very weak, might have a nice meal."

"And where does your grandmother live?" asked the wolf.

"Oh, about twenty minutes' walk further into the wood. Her house stands under three great oak trees. And nearby are some nut trees which you must know."

The wolf was thinking to himself, She is a nice tender thing, and will taste better than the old woman. I must act cleverly, that I may make a meal of both.

He walked along with Red Riding Hood for a while, then he said, "Look at the pretty flowers, Red Riding Hood. Why don't you look about you? I don't believe you even hear the birds sing. You are just as solemn as if you were going to school. Everything is so gay out here in the wood."

Red Riding Hood raised her eyes, and when she saw the sunlight dancing through the trees, and all the bright flowers, she thought: I'm sure Grannie would be pleased if I took her a bunch of fresh flowers. It is still quite early. I shall have plenty of time to pick them."

So she left the path, and wandered off among the trees to pick the flowers. Each time she picked one, she always saw another prettier one further on. So she went deeper and deeper into the forest.

In the meantime, the wolf went straight off to the grandmother's cottage, and knocked at the door.

"Who is there?"

"Red Riding Hood, bringing you meat and some wine. Open the door!"

"Press the latch!" cried the old woman. "I am too weak to get up."

The wolf pressed the latch, and the door sprang open. He went straight in and up to the bed without saying a word, and ate up the poor old woman. Then he put on her nightdress and nightcap, got into bed and drew the curtains.

Red Riding Hood ran about picking flowers until she could carry no more. Then she remembered her grandmother again. She was astonished when she got to the house to find the door open. When she entered the room everything seemed so strange.

She felt quite frightened, but she did not know why. Generally I like coming to see grandmother so much, she thought. She cried, "Good morning, Grandmother," but she received no answer.

Then she went up to the bed and drew the curtain back. There lay her grandmother but she had drawn her cap down over her face, and she looked very odd.

"Oh, Grandmother, what big ears you have," she said.

"The better to hear you with, my dear."

"Grandmother, what big eyes you have."

"The better to see you with, my dear."

"What big hands you have, Grandmother."

"The better to catch hold of you with, my dear."

"But Grandmother, what big teeth you have."

"The better to eat you with, my dear."

Hardly had the wolf said this, than he sprang out of bed, and devoured poor little Red Riding Hood. Then the wolf went back to bed and was soon snoring loudly.

A hunter went past the house, and thought, How loudly the old lady is snoring; I must see if there is anything the matter with her.

So he went into the house, and up to the bed, where he found the wolf

fast asleep. "Do I find you here, you old sinner?" he said. "Long enough have I sought you."

He raised his gun to shoot, when it just occurred to him that perhaps the wolf had eaten the old lady, and that she might still be saved. So he took a knife and began cutting open the sleeping Wolf. At the first cut he saw the little red cloak, and after a few more slashes, the little girl sprang out, and cried, "Oh, how frightened I was. It was so dark inside the wolf!" Next the old grandmother came out, alive, but hardly able to breathe.

Red Riding Hood brought some big stones with which they filled the wolf, so that when he woke and tried to spring away, they dragged him back, and he fell down dead.

They were all quite happy now. The huntsman skinned the wolf, and took the skin home. The grandmother ate the cake and drank the wine which Red Riding Hood had brought, and she soon felt quite strong. And Red Riding Hood thought, I will never again wander off into the forest as long as I live, if my mother forbids it.

Snow White and Rose Red

A poor widow once lived in a little cottage with a garden in front of it, in which grew two rose trees, one bearing white roses and the other red. She had two children, who were just like the two rose trees. One was called Snow White and the other Rose Red. They were the sweetest and best children in the world, always diligent and always cheerful, but Snow White was quieter and more gentle thàn Rose Red. Rose Red loved to run about the fields and meadows and to pick flowers and catch butterflies, but Snow White sat at home with her mother and helped her in the household, or read aloud to her when there was no work to do.

The two children loved each other so dearly that they always walked hand in hand whenever they went out together. When Snow White said, "We will never desert each other," Rose Red answered, "No, not as long as we live," and the mother added, "Whatever one gets she shall share with the other."

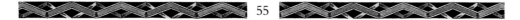

They often roamed about in the woods gathering berries and no beast tried to hurt them. On the contrary, they came up to them in the most confiding manner. The little hare would eat a cabbage leaf from their hands, the deer grazed beside them, the stag would bound past them merrily, and the birds remained on the branches and sang to them with all their might. No evil ever befell them. If they tarried late in the wood and night overtook them, they lay down together on the moss and slept until morning, and their mother knew they were quite safe and never felt anxious about them.

Once, when they had slept the night in the wood and had been wakened by the morning sun, they perceived a beautiful child in a shining white robe sitting close to their resting place. The figure got up, looked at them kindly, but said nothing and vanished into the wood. And when they looked around them they became aware that they had slept quite close to a precipice, over which they would certainly have fallen had they gone on a few steps further in the darkness. When they told their mother of their adventure, she said what they had seen must have been the angel that guards good children.

Snow White and Rose Red kept their mother's cottage so beautifully clean and neat that it was a pleasure to go into it. In summer Rose Red looked after the house, and every morning before her mother awoke she placed a bunch of flowers, including a rose from each tree, near the bed. In winter Snow White lit the fire and put on the kettle, which was made of brass, but so beautifully polished that it shone like gold. In the evening when the snowflakes fell their mother said, "Snow White, go and close the shutters." And they drew around the fire, while their mother put on her spectacles and read aloud from a big book, and the two girls listened and sat and spun. Beside them on the ground lay a little lamb, and behind them perched a little white dove, its head tucked under its wings.

One evening as they sat thus cozily together someone knocked at the door as though he desired admittance. The mother said, "Rose Red, open the door quickly. It must be a traveler seeking shelter."

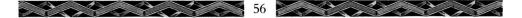

Rose Red hurried to unbar the door. She thought she saw a poor man standing in the darkness outside, but it was no such thing. It was a bear, who poked his thick black head through the door. Rose Red screamed and sprang back in terror. The lamb began to bleat. The dove flapped its wings. And Snow White ran and hid behind her mother's bed.

But the bear began to speak, and said, "Don't be afraid. I won't hurt you. I am half frozen, and only wish to warm myself a little."

"My poor bear," said the mother, "lie down by the fire, only take care you don't burn your fur." Then she called out, "Snow White and Rose Red, come out. The bear will do you no harm. He is a good, honest creature."

So they both came out from their hiding places, and gradually the lamb and dove drew near, too, and they all forgot their fear. The bear asked the children to beat the snow a little out of his fur, and they fetched a brush and scrubbed him until he was dry. Then the beast stretched himself in front of the fire and growled quite happily and comfortably. The children soon grew quite at their ease with him. They tugged his fur with their hands, put their small feet on his back, and rolled him about here and there, or took a hazel wand and beat him with it. And when he growled

they only laughed. The bear submitted to everything with the best possible good nature; only when they went too far he cried,

"Oh! children, spare my life!
Snow White and Rose Red,
Don't beat your lover dead."

When it was time to retire for the night and the others went to bed, the mother said to the bear, "You can lie there on the hearth. It will be shelter for you from the cold and wet." As soon as day dawned the children let him out, and he trotted over the snow into the wood.

From this time on the bear came every evening at the same hour, and lay down by the hearth and let the children play what pranks they liked with him. They got so accustomed to him that the door was never shut until their furry friend had made his appearance.

When spring came and all outside was green, the bear said one morning to Snow White, "Now I must go away and not return again the whole summer."

"Where are you going, dear bear?" asked Snow White.

"I must go to the wood and protect my treasure from the wicked dwarfs. In winter, when the earth is frozen hard, they are obliged to remain underground, for they can't work their way through. But now, when the sun has thawed and warmed the ground, they break through and come up above to steal what they can. What once falls into their hands and into their caves is not easily brought back to light."

Snow White was quite sad about their friend's departure. When she unbarred the door for him the bear, stepping out, caught a piece of fur in the door knocker. Snow White thought she caught sight of glittering gold beneath it, but she couldn't be certain of it. And the bear ran hastily away and soon disappeared behind the trees.

A short time after this the mother sent the children into the forest to collect wood for their fireplace. In their wanderings they came upon a big tree which lay felled on the ground. On the trunk, among the long grass,

they saw something jumping up and down, but what it was they couldn't distinguish. When they drew nearer they saw a dwarf with a wizened face and a beard a yard long. The end of the beard was jammed into a cleft of the tree, and the little man sprang about like a dog on a chain, and didn't seem to know what he was to do.

He glared at the girls with his fiery red eyes and screamed, "What are you standing there for? Can't you come and help me?"

"What were you doing, little man?" asked Rose Red.

"You stupid, inquisitive goose!" replied the dwarf. "I wanted to split the tree, to get little chips of wood for our kitchen fire. Those thick logs that serve to make fires for coarse, greedy people like yourselves burn up all the little food we need. I had successfully driven in the wedge and all was going well, but the wood was so slippery that it suddenly sprang out, and the tree closed up so rapidly that I had no time to take my beautiful white beard out. So here I am stuck fast and I can't get away. And you silly, smooth-faced, milk-and-water girls just stand and laugh! Ugh! what wretches you are!"

The children did all in their power, but they couldn't get the beard out. It was wedged in far too firmly. "I will run and fetch somebody," said Rose Red.

"Crazy blockheads!" snapped the dwarf. "What's the good of calling anyone else? You're already too many for me. Does nothing better occur to you than that?"

"Don't be so impatient," said Snow White. "I'll help you." And taking her scissors out of her pocket she cut the end off his beard. As soon as the dwarf felt himself free he seized a bag full of gold which was hidden among the roots of the tree, lifted it up, and muttered aloud, "Drat these rude wretches, cutting off a piece of my splendid beard!" With these words he swung the bag over his back and disappeared without as much as looking at the children again.

Shortly after this Snow White and Rose Red went out to get some fish for dinner. As they approached the stream they saw something which

looked like an enormous grasshopper springing toward the water as if it were going to jump in. They ran forward and recognized their old friend the dwarf.

"Where are you going to?" asked Rose Red. "You're surely not going to jump into the water?"

"I'm not such a fool," screamed the dwarf. "Don't you see that fish is trying to drag me in?"

The little man had been sitting on the bank fishing, when unfortunately the wind had entangled his beard in the line. When immediately afterward a big fish bit, the feeble little creature had no strength to pull it out. The fish dragged the dwarf toward him. With all his might the dwarf clung to every rush and blade of grass, but it didn't help him much. He had to follow every movement of the fish and was in great danger of being drawn into the water.

The girls came up just at the right moment, held him firm, and did all they could to disentangle his beard from the line. But in vain—beard and line were in a hopeless muddle. Nothing remained but to produce the scissors and cut the beard, by which a small part of it was sacrificed.

When the dwarf perceived what they were about he yelled to them, "Do you call that manners, you toadstools, to disfigure a fellow's face? It wasn't enough that you shortened my beard before, but you must now cut off the best of it. I can't appear like this before my own people." Then he fetched a sack of pearls that lay among the rushes, and without saying another word he dragged it away and disappeared behind a stone.

It happened that soon after this the mother sent the two girls to the town to buy needles, thread, laces, and ribbons. Their road led over a heath where huge rocks lay scattered here and there. While trudging along they saw a big bird hovering in the air, circling slowly above them, but always descending lower, till at last it settled on a rock not far from them. Immediately afterward they heard a sharp, piercing cry. They ran forward and saw with horror that the eagle had pounced on their old friend the dwarf and was about to carry him off. The tender-hearted children seized hold of the little man, and struggled so long with the bird that at last he let go of his prey.

When the dwarf had recovered from the first shock he screamed in his screeching voice, "Couldn't you have treated me more carefully? You have torn my thin little coat all to shreds, useless, awkward hussies that you are!" Then he took a bag of precious stones and vanished under the rocks into his cave.

The girls were accustomed to his ingratitude, and went on their way and did their business in town. On their way home, as they were again passing the heath, they surprised the dwarf pouring out his precious stones on an open space, for he had thought no one would pass by at so late an hour. The evening sun shone on the glittering stones, and they

gleamed so beautifully that the children stood still and gazed on them.

"What are you standing there gaping for?" screamed the dwarf, and his ashen-gray face became scarlet with rage. He was about to go off with these angry words, when a sudden growl was heard and a black bear trotted out of the wood. The dwarf jumped up in a great fright, but he hadn't time to reach his place of retreat, for the bear was already close to him. Then he cried in terror, "Dear Mr. Bear, spare me! I'll give you all my treasure. Look at these beautiful precious stones lying there. Spare my life! What pleasure would you get from a poor feeble little fellow like me? You won't feel me between your teeth. There, lay hold of these two wicked girls—they will be a tender morsel for you as fat as young quails. Eat them up, for heaven's sake."

But the bear, paying no attention to his words, gave the evil little creature one blow with his paw and he never moved again.

The girls had run away, but the bear called after them, "Snow White and Rose Red, don't be afraid. Wait, and I'll come with you." Then they recognized his voice and stood still, and when the bear was quite close to them his skin suddenly fell off, and a beautiful man stood beside them, all dressed in gold.

"I am a king's son," he said, "and have been doomed by that unholy little dwarf, who had stolen my treasure, to roam about the woods as a wild bear till his death should set me free. Now he has got his well-merited punishment."

Snow White married the prince and Rose Red married his brother, and they divided between them the great treasure the dwarf had collected in his cave. The old mother lived peacefully with her children for many years. She brought the two rose trees with her, and they stood in front of her window, and every year they bore the finest red and white roses.

The Sleeping Beauty

O nce upon a time there lived a king and queen who had no children and this they lamented very much. But one day, as the queen was walking by the side of the river, a little fish lifted its head out of the water, and said, "Your wish shall be fulfilled, and you shall soon have a daughter."

What the little fish had foretold soon came to pass. The queen had a little girl who was so very beautiful that the king could not cease looking on her for joy. He decided to have a great feast and he invited not only his relations, friends, and neighbors, but also all the fairies, that they might be kind and good to his little daughter. Now there were thirteen fairies in his kingdom, and he had only twelve golden dishes for them to eat from, so he was obliged to leave one of the fairies without an invitation. The rest came, and after the feast was over they each gave their best gift to the little princess. One gave her virtue, another beauty, another riches. One gave her the wit of an angel, another said she would have grace in everything she did, another said she would sing like a nightingale. When eleven of the fairies had blessed her, the thirteenth, who had not been invited, and was very angry on that account, came in, determined to take her revenge. She cried out, "The king's daughter shall in her fifteenth year be wounded by a spindle, and fall down dead."

Then the twelfth fairy, who had not yet given her gift, came forward and said that the bad wish must be fulfilled, but that she could soften it, and that the king's daughter would not die, but would sleep for a hundred years.

But the king hoped to save his dear child from the threatened evil, and ordered that all the spindles in the kingdom should be destroyed. In the

meantime, all the fairies' gifts were fulfilled. The princess was so beautiful, and well-behaved, and amiable, and wise, that everyone who knew her loved her.

Now it happened that on the very day she was fifteen years old the king and queen were not at home, and she was left alone in the palace. So she roamed about by herself, and looked at all the rooms and chambers, until at last she came to a narrow staircase that led to a little door. In the door there was a golden key, and when she turned it the door sprang open. There in a little room at the top of a tower sat an old lady spinning away very busily.

"What are you doing there?" asked the princess.

"Spinning," said the old lady, and nodded her head.

"How prettily that little thing turns round!" said the princess. "Please

let me try it." She took the spindle and began to spin. But scarcely had she touched it before the prophecy was fulfilled, and she fell down, as if lifeless, on the ground.

But she was not dead. She had only fallen into a deep sleep. The king and queen, who just then came home, and all their court, fell asleep too. The horses slept in the stables, and the dogs in the court, the pigeons on the house top, and the flies on the walls. Even the fire in the hearth stopped blazing and went to sleep. And the meat that was roasting stood still. The cook, who was at that moment pulling the kitchen boy by the hair to give him a box on the ear for something he had done amiss, let him go, and both fell asleep. And so everything in the palace stood still and slept soundly.

Soon a large hedge of thorns grew around the palace. Every year it became higher and thicker, until at last the whole palace was surrounded and hidden, so that not even the roof or the chimneys could be seen. But throughout the land there were stories of the beautiful sleeping Briar Rose (for so was the king's daughter called) so that from time to time several princes came and tried to break through the thicket into the palace. This they could never do for the thorns and bushes laid hold of them, and there they stuck fast and died miserably.

After many years yet another king's son came to that kingdom. An old man told him the story of the thicket of thorns, and how a beautiful palace stood behind it, in which there was a wondrous princess, called Briar Rose, asleep with all her court. He told, too, how he had heard from his grandfather that many, many princes had tried to break through the thicket, but had stuck fast and died.

The young prince said, "All this does not frighten me. I will go and see Briar Rose." The old man tried to dissuade him, but he persisted in going.

Now that very day the hundred years were completed. As the prince came to the thicket he saw nothing but beautiful flowering shrubs, through which he passed with ease, but they closed after him, as firm as

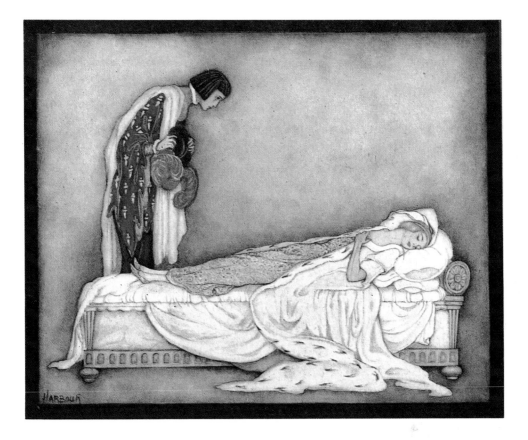

ever. Then he came at last to the palace. There in the court lay the dogs asleep, and the horses were asleep in the stables. On the roof sat the pigeons fast asleep with their heads under their wings. When he came into the palace, he saw the flies asleep on the walls, and the cook in the kitchen still holding up her hand as if she would hit the boy, and the maid with her pail in her hand was going a-milking.

Then he went on still further. All was so quiet that he could hear every breath he drew. At last he came to the old tower and opened the door to the little room. There lay Briar Rose fast asleep. She looked so beautiful that he could not turn his eyes away, and he stooped down and gave her

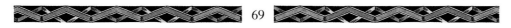

a kiss. The moment he kissed her she opened her eyes, and smiled upon him. For the spell was broken.

They went out together, and presently the king and queen also awoke, and all the court, and they gazed at each other with great wonder. And the horses got up and shook themselves, and the dogs jumped about and barked. The pigeons took their heads from under their wings, and looked around and flew into the fields. The flies on the walls buzzed. The fire in the kitchen blazed up and cooked the dinner, and the roast meat turned round again. The cook gave the boy the box on his ear so that he cried out, and the maid went to milk the cows.

And then the wedding of the prince and Briar Rose was celebrated, and they lived happily together all their lives long.

The White Cat

There was once a king who had three sons. They were all so clever and brave that he began to be afraid that they would want to reign over the kingdom before he was dead. Now the king, although he felt that he was growing old, wished to continue to rule his kingdom while he could still manage it very well. He thought the best way to live in peace would be to divert the minds of his sons by promises which he could always get out of when the time came for keeping them.

So he sent for his three sons. After speaking to them kindly he added, "You will quite agree with me, my dear children, that my great age makes it impossible for me to look after my affairs of state as carefully as I once did. I begin to fear that this may affect the welfare of my subjects; therefore I wish that one of you should succeed to my crown. But in

return for such a gift as this it is only right that you should do something for me. Now, as I think of retiring into the country, it seems to me that a pretty, lively, faithful little dog would be very good company for me. So, without any regard for your ages, I promise that the one who brings me the most beautiful little dog shall succeed me at once."

The three princes were greatly surprised by their father's sudden fancy for a little dog, but since it gave the two younger ones a chance they would not otherwise have had of being king, and since the eldest was too polite to make any objection, they accepted the commission with pleasure. They bade farewell to the king, who gave them presents of silver and precious stones and appointed to meet them at the same hour, in the same place, after a year had passed, to see the little dogs they had brought for him.

The princes went together to a castle which was about a league from the city. They were accompanied by all their friends, to whom they gave a grand banquet. Then the three brothers promised to be friends always, to share whatever good fortune befell them, and not to be parted by any envy or jealousy. And so they set out, agreeing to meet at the same castle at the appointed time, to present themselves before the king together. Each one took a different road, and the two eldest met with many adventures, but it is about the youngest that you are going to hear. He was young and happy and handsome, and knew everything that a prince ought to know. And as for his courage, there was simply no end to it.

Hardly a day passed without the prince buying several dogs—big and little, greyhounds, mastiffs, spaniels, and lapdogs. As soon as he had bought a pretty one he was sure to see one still prettier. Then he had to get rid of all the others and buy that one, since, being alone, he found it impossible to take thirty or forty thousand dogs about with him. He journeyed from day to day, not knowing where he was going, until at last, just at nightfall, he reached a great, gloomy forest.

He did not know his way, and to make matters worse it began to thunder and the rain poured down. He took the first path he could find, and after

walking for a long time he thought he saw a faint light, and began to hope that he was coming to some cottage where he might find shelter for the night. At length, guided by the light, he reached the door of the most splendid castle he could have imagined. This door was of gold covered with large rubies, and it was the pure red light which shone from them that had shown him the way through the forest. The walls were of the finest porcelain in the most delicate colors, and the prince saw that all the stories he had ever read were pictured upon them. But since he was terribly wet and the rain still fell in torrents, he could not stay to look about any more, but came back to the golden door. There he saw a deer's foot hanging by a chain of diamonds, and he began to wonder who could live in this magnificent castle.

"They must feel very secure against robbers," he said to himself. "What is to hinder anyone from cutting off that chain and digging out those rubies and making himself rich for life?"

He pulled the deer's foot, and immediately a silver bell sounded and the door flew open. But the prince could see nothing but many hands in the air, each holding a torch. He was so surprised that he stood quite still, until he felt himself pushed forward by other hands, so that though he was somewhat uneasy, he could not help going on. With his hand on his sword, to be prepared for whatever might happen, he entered a hall paved with lapis lazuli, while two lovely voices sang:

> "The hands you see floating above
>   Will swiftly your bidding obey;
> If your heart dreads not conquering love,
>   In this place you may fearlessly stay."

The prince could not believe that any danger threatened him when he was welcomed in this way, as, guided by the mysterious hands, he went toward a door of coral, which opened of its own accord. He found himself in a vast hall of mother-of-pearl, out of which opened a number of other rooms, glittering with thousands of lights and full of such beau-

tiful pictures and precious things that the prince felt quite bewildered. After passing through sixty rooms, the hands that conducted him stopped, and the prince saw a most comfortable-looking armchair drawn up close to the chimney corner. At the same moment the fire lighted itself, and pretty, soft, clever hands took off the prince's wet, muddy clothes and presented him with fresh ones made of the richest stuffs, all embroidered with gold and emeralds. He could not help admiring everything he saw and the deft way in which the hands waited on him, though they sometimes appeared so suddenly that they made him jump.

When he was quite ready—and looked very different from the wet and weary prince who had stood outside in the rain and pulled the deer's foot—the hands led him to a splendid room, upon the walls of which were painted the histories of Puss in Boots and a number of other famous cats. The table was laid for supper with two golden plates, and golden spoons and forks, and the sideboard was covered with dishes and glasses of crystal set with precious stones. The prince was wondering who the second place could be for, when suddenly in came about a dozen cats carrying guitars and rolls of music. They took their places at one end of the room and, under the direction of a cat who beat time with a roll of paper, began to mew in every imaginable key and to draw their claws across the strings of the guitars, making the strangest music that could be heard. The prince hastily stopped up his ears, but even then the sight of these comical musicians sent him into fits of laughter.

"What funny thing shall I see next?" he said to himself, and instantly the door opened and in came a tiny figure covered by a long black veil. It was conducted by two cats wearing black mantles and carrying swords, and a large party of cats followed.

The prince was so astonished that he thought he must be dreaming, but the little figure came up to him and threw back its veil, and he saw that it was the loveliest little white cat. She looked very young and very sad, and in a sweet little voice that went straight to his heart she said to him, "King's Son, you are welcome. The queen of the cats is glad to see you."

"Lady Cat," replied the prince, "I thank you for receiving me so kindly, but surely you are no ordinary pussycat? Indeed, the way you speak and the magnificence of your castle prove it plainly."

"King's Son," said the white cat, "I beg you to spare me these compliments, for I am not used to them. But now," she added, "let supper be served and let the musicians be silent, since the prince does not understand what they are saying."

So the mysterious hands began to bring in the supper. First they put on the table two dishes, one containing stewed pigeons and the other a fricassee of fat mice. The sight of the latter made the prince feel as if he could not enjoy his supper at all. But the white cat seeing this assured him that the dishes intended for him were prepared in a separate kitchen, and he might be certain that they contained neither rats nor mice. The prince felt so sure that she would not deceive him that he had no more hesitation in beginning.

Presently he noticed that on the little paw that was next to him the white cat wore a bracelet containing a portrait, and he begged to be allowed to look at it. To his great surprise he found it represented an extremely handsome young man, who was so like himself that it might have been his own portrait! The white cat sighed as he looked at it and seemed sadder than ever, and the prince dared not ask any questions for fear of displeasing her. So he began to talk about other things, and found that she was interested in all the subjects he cared for himself, and seemed to know quite well what was going on in the world.

After supper they went into another room, which was fitted up as a theater, and the cats acted and danced for their amusement. Then the white cat said good night to him, and the hands conducted him into a room he had not seen before, hung with tapestry worked with butterflies' wings of every color. There were mirrors that reached from the ceiling to the floor, and a little white bed with curtains of gauze tied up with ribbons. The prince went to bed in silence, since he did not know how to begin a conversation with the hands that waited on him.

In the morning he was awakened by noise and confusion outside his window, and the hands came and quickly dressed him in hunting costume. When he looked out all the cats were assembled in the courtyard, some leading greyhounds, some blowing horns, for the white cat was going hunting.

The hands led a wooden horse up to the prince and seemed to expect him to mount it, at which he was very indignant. But it was no use for him to object, for he speedily found himself upon its back, and it pranced gaily off with him.

The white cat herself was riding a monkey, which climbed up to the eagles' nests when she had a fancy for the young eaglets. Never was there a pleasanter hunting party. When they returned to the castle the prince and the white cat supped together as before, but when they had finished she offered him a crystal goblet, which must have contained a magic draught, for as soon as he had swallowed its contents he forgot everything, even the little dog that he was seeking for the king, and only thought how happy he was to be with the white cat! And so the days passed, in every kind of amusement, until the year was nearly gone.

The prince had forgotten all about meeting his brothers. He did not even know what country he belonged to. But the white cat knew when he ought to go back, and one day she said to him, "Do you know that you have only three days left to look for the little dog for your father? Your brothers have found lovely ones."

The prince suddenly recovered his memory and cried, "What can have made me forget such an important thing? My whole fortune depends upon it. And even if I could in such a short time find a dog pretty enough to gain me a kingdom, where should I find a horse who could carry me all that way in three days?" And he began to be very vexed.

But the white cat said to him, "King's Son, do not trouble yourself. I am your friend and will make everything easy for you. You can still stay here for a day, since the good wooden horse can take you to your country in twelve hours."

"I thank you, beautiful cat," said the prince, "but what good will it do me to get back if I have not a dog to take to my father?"

"See here," answered the white cat, holding up an acorn. "There is a prettier one in this than in the dog star!"

"Oh! White Cat dear," said the prince, "how unkind you are to laugh at me now!"

"Only listen," she said, holding the acorn to his ear.

And inside it he distinctly heard a tiny voice say, "Bow-wow!"

The prince was delighted, for a dog that can be shut up in an acorn must be very small indeed. He wanted to take it out and look at it, but the white cat said it would be better not to open the acorn until he was before the king, in case the tiny dog should be cold on the journey. He thanked her a thousand times, and said goodbye quite sadly when the time came for him to set out.

"The days have passed so quickly with you," he said, "I only wish I could take you with me now."

But the white cat shook her head and sighed deeply in reply.

The prince was the first to arrive at the castle where he had agreed to meet his brothers, but they came soon after and stared in amazement when they saw the wooden horse in the courtyard jumping like a hunter.

The prince met them joyfully, and they began to tell him all their adventures. But he managed to hide from them what he had been doing, and even led them to think that a turnspit dog which he had with him was the one he was bringing for the king. Fond as they all were of one another, the two eldest could not help being glad to think that their dogs certainly had a better chance.

The next morning they started in the same chariot. The elder brothers carried in baskets two dogs so tiny and fragile that they hardly dared touch them. As for the turnspit, he ran after the chariot, and got so covered with mud that one could hardly see what he was like at all.

When they reached the palace everyone crowded round to welcome the princes as they went into the king's great hall. When the two brothers

presented their little dogs nobody could decide which was the prettier. They were already arranging between themselves to share the kingdom equally, when the youngest stepped forward, drawing from his pocket the acorn the white cat had given him. He opened it quickly, and there upon a white cushion they saw a dog so small that it could easily have been put through a ring. The prince laid it upon the ground, and it got up at once and began to dance. The king did not know what to say, for it was impossible that anything could be prettier than this little creature. Nevertheless, as he was in no hurry to part with his crown, he told his sons that, since they had been so successful the first time, he would ask them to go once again, and seek by land and sea a piece of muslin so fine that it could be drawn through the eye of a needle.

The brothers were not very willing to set out again, but the two eldest consented because it gave them another chance, and they started as before. The youngest again mounted the wooden horse and rode back at full speed to his beloved white cat.

Every door of the castle stood wide open and every window and turret was illuminated, so it looked more wonderful than before. The hands hastened to meet him and led the wooden horse off to the stable, while he hurried in to find the white cat. She was asleep in a little basket on a white satin cushion, but she awoke when she heard the prince, and was overjoyed at seeing him once more.

"How could I hope that you would come back to me, King's Son?" she said. And then he stroked and petted her, and told her of his successful journey, and how he had come back to ask her help, since he believed that it was impossible to find what the king demanded.

The white cat looked serious and said she must think about what was to be done, but that, luckily, there were some cats in the castle who could spin very well, and if anybody could manage it they could, and she would set them the task herself.

And then the hands appeared carrying torches, and conducted the prince and the white cat to a long gallery which overlooked the river. From the windows they saw a magnificent display of fireworks. Afterward they had supper, which the prince liked even better than the fireworks, for it was very late and he was hungry after his long ride. And so the days passed as quickly as before.

It was impossible to feel dull with the white cat, and she had quite a talent for inventing new amusements—indeed, she was cleverer than a cat has any right to be. But when the prince asked her how it was that she was so wise she only said, "King's Son, do not ask me. Guess what you please. I may not tell you anything."

The prince was so happy that he did not trouble himself at all about the

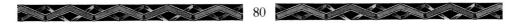

time, but presently the white cat told him that the year was gone, and that he need not be at all anxious about the piece of muslin, as they had made it very well.

"This time," she added, "I can give you a suitable escort." Looking out into the courtyard the prince saw a superb chariot of burnished gold, enameled in flame color. It was drawn by twelve snow-white horses, harnessed four abreast. Their trappings were of flame-colored velvet, embroidered with diamonds. A hundred chariots followed, each drawn by eight horses and filled with officers in splendid uniforms, and a thousand guards surrounded the procession.

"Go!" said the white cat, "and when you appear before the king in such state he surely will not refuse you the crown which you deserve. Take this walnut, but do not open it until you are before him. Then you will find in it the piece of muslin you asked me for."

"Lovely Blanchette," said the prince, "how can I thank you properly for all your kindness to me? Only tell me that you wish it, and I will give up forever all thought of being king and will stay here with you always."

"King's Son," she replied, "it shows the goodness of your heart that you should care so much for a little white cat who is good for nothing but to catch mice. But you must not stay."

So the prince kissed her little paw and set out. They reached the king's palace in just half the time it had taken the wooden horse to get there. This time, however, the prince was so late that he did not try to meet his brothers at their castle. They thought he could not be coming and were rather glad of it, and displayed their pieces of muslin to the king proudly, feeling sure of success. And indeed the material was very fine and would go through the eye of a very large needle. But the king, who was only too glad to make a difficulty, sent for a particular needle, which was kept among the crown jewels and had such a small eye that everybody saw at once that it was impossible that the muslin should pass through it.

The princes were angry and were beginning to complain that it was a trick, when suddenly the trumpets sounded and the youngest prince came

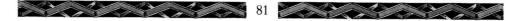

in. His father and brothers were quite astonished at his magnificence, and after he had greeted them he took the walnut from his pocket and opened it, fully expecting to find the piece of muslin. But instead there was only a hazel nut. He cracked it, and there lay a cherry stone. Everybody was looking on, and the king was chuckling to himself at the idea of finding the piece of muslin in a nutshell.

The prince, however, cracked the cherry stone, but everyone laughed when he saw it contained only its own kernel. He opened that and found a grain of wheat, and in that was a millet seed. Then he himself began to wonder, and muttered softly, "White Cat, White Cat, are you making fun of me?"

In an instant he felt a cat's claw give his hand quite a sharp scratch, and hoping that it was meant as encouragement he opened the millet seed and drew out of it a piece of muslin four hundred ells long. It was woven with the loveliest colors and most wonderful patterns and when the needle was brought it went through the eye six times with the greatest ease! The king turned pale and the other princes stood silent and sorrowful, for nobody could deny that this was the most marvelous piece of muslin that was to be found in the world.

Presently the king turned to his sons and said, with a deep sigh, "Nothing could console me more in my old age than to realize your willingness to gratify my wishes. Go then once more, and whoever at the end of a year can bring back the loveliest princess shall be married to her, and shall, without further delay, receive the crown, for my successor must certainly be married."

The youngest prince considered that he had earned the kingdom fairly twice over, but he was too well-bred to argue about it, so he just went back to his gorgeous chariot, and, surrounded by his escort, returned to the white cat faster than he had come.

This time she was expecting him. The path was strewn with flowers and a thousand braziers were burning scented wood which perfumed the air. Seated in a gallery from which she could see his arrival, the white cat waited for him.

"Well, King's Son," she said, "here you are once more, without a crown."

"Madam," said he, "thanks to your generosity I have earned one twice over. But the fact is that my father is so loath to part with it that it would be no pleasure to me to take it."

"Never mind," she answered. "It's just as well to try to deserve it. As you must take back a lovely princess with you next time, I will look for one for you. In the meantime let us enjoy ourselves. Tonight, to amuse you, I have ordered a battle between my cats and the river rats."

So this year slipped away even more pleasantly than the preceding

ones. Sometimes the prince could not help asking the white cat how it was she could talk.

"Perhaps you are a fairy," he said. "Or has some enchanter changed you into a cat?"

But she only gave him answers that told him nothing. Days go by so quickly when one is very happy that it is certain the prince would never have thought of its being time to go back, when one evening as they sat together the white cat told him that if he wanted to take a lovely princess home with him the next day he must be prepared to do as she said.

"Take this sword," she said, "and cut off my head!"

"I cannot cut off your head!" cried the prince. "Blanchette darling, how could I do it?"

"I entreat you to do as I tell you, King's Son," she replied.

The tears came into the prince's eyes as he begged her to ask him anything but that—to set him any task she pleased as a proof of his devotion, but to spare him the grief of killing his dear pussycat. But nothing he could say altered her determination, and at last he drew his sword, and desperately, with a trembling hand, cut off the little white head. Imagine his astonishment and delight when suddenly a lovely princess stood before him, and, while he was still speechless with amazement, the door opened and a goodly company of knights and ladies entered, each carrying a cat's skin! They hastened with every sign of joy to the princess, kissing her hand and congratulating her on being once more restored to her natural shape. She received them graciously, but after a few minutes begged that they would leave her alone with the prince.

Then she said to him, "You see, Prince, that you were right in supposing me to be no ordinary cat. My father reigned over six kingdoms. The queen, my mother, whom he loved dearly, had a passion for traveling and exploring. When I was only a few weeks old she obtained his permission to visit a certain mountain of which she had heard many marvelous tales, and set out, taking with her a number of her attendants. On the way they had to pass near an old castle belonging to the fairies.

Nobody had ever been into it, but it was reported to be full of the most wonderful things. My mother remembered hearing that the fairies had in their garden such fruits as were to be seen and tasted nowhere else. She began to wish to try for herself, and turned her steps in the direction of the garden. On arriving at the door, which blazed with gold and jewels, she ordered her servants to knock loudly. But it was useless. It seemed as if all the inhabitants of the castle must be asleep or dead. Now, the more difficult it became to obtain the fruit, the more the queen was determined that have it she would. So she ordered that they bring ladders and get over the wall into the garden. But though the wall did not look very high, and they tied the ladders together to make them very long, it was quite impossible to get to the top.

"The queen was in despair, but as night was coming on she ordered that they should encamp just where they were, and went to bed herself, feeling quite ill, she was so disappointed. In the middle of the night she was suddenly awakened, and saw to her surprise a tiny, ugly old woman seated by her bedside, who said to her, 'I must say that we consider it somewhat troublesome of Your Majesty to insist upon tasting our fruit, but to save you any annoyance, my sisters and I will consent to give you as much as you can carry away on one condition—that is, that you shall give us your little daughter to bring up as our own.'

" 'Ah! my dear madam,' cried the queen, 'is there nothing else that you will take for the fruit? I will give you my kingdoms willingly.'

" 'No,' replied the old fairy, 'we will have nothing but your little daughter. She shall be as happy as the day is long, and we will give her everything that is worth having in Fairyland, but you must not see her again until she is married.'

" 'Though it is a hard condition,' said the queen, 'I consent, for I shall certainly die if I do not taste the fruit, and so I should lose my little daughter either way.'

"So the old fairy led her into the castle, and though it was still the middle of the night, the queen could see plainly that it was far more

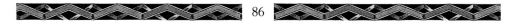

beautiful than she had been told, which you can easily believe, Prince," said the white cat, "when I tell you that it was this castle that we are now in. 'Will you gather the fruit yourself, queen?' said the old fairy, 'or shall I call it to come to you?'

" 'I beg you to let me see it come when it is called,' cried the queen. 'That will be something quite new.' The old fairy whistled twice, then she cried, 'Apricots, peaches, nectarines, cherries, plums, pears, melons, grapes, apples, oranges, lemons, strawberries, raspberries, come!'

"And in an instant they came tumbling in, one over another, and yet they were neither dusty nor spoiled, and the queen found them quite as good as she had fancied them. You see, they grew upon fairy trees.

"The old fairy gave her golden baskets in which to take the fruit away, and it was as much as four hundred mules could carry. Then she reminded the queen of her agreement and led her back to the camp.

"The next morning, the queen went back to her kingdom; but before she had gone very far she began to repent of her bargain. When the king came out to meet her she looked so sad that he guessed that something had happened, and asked what was the matter. At first the queen was afraid to tell him, but when, as soon as they reached the palace, five frightful little dwarfs were sent by the fairies to fetch me, she was obliged to confess what she had promised.

"The king was very angry, and had the queen and myself shut up in a great tower and safely guarded. He drove the little dwarfs out of his kingdom. But the fairies sent a great dragon who ate up all the people he met, and whose breath burned up everything as he passed through the country. At last, after trying in vain to rid himself of the monster, the king, to save his subjects, was obliged to consent that I should be given up to the fairies. This time they came themselves to fetch me, in a chariot of pearl drawn by seahorses followed by the dragon, who was led with chains of diamonds.

"My cradle was placed between the old fairies, who kissed and caressed me, and away we whirled through the air to a tower which they had built

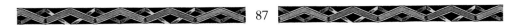

specially for me. There I grew up surrounded with everything that was beautiful and rare and learning everything that is ever taught to a princess, but without any companions, except a parrot and a little dog, who could both talk, and receiving every day a visit from one of the old fairies, who came mounted upon a dragon.

"One day, however, as I sat at my window I saw a handsome young prince, who seemed to have been hunting in the forest which surrounded my prison, and who was standing and looking up at me. When he saw that I observed him he saluted me with great deference. You can imagine that I was delighted to have someone new to talk to, and in spite of the height of my window our conversation was prolonged until night fell; then my prince reluctantly bade me farewell. But after that he came again many times, and at last I consented to marry him, but the question was how was I to escape from my tower.

"The fairies always supplied me with flax for my spinning, and by great diligence I made enough cord for a ladder that would reach to the foot of the tower. But, alas! just as my prince was helping me to descend it, the crossest and ugliest of the old fairies flew in. Before he had time to defend himself my unhappy lover was swallowed up by the dragon. As for me, the fairies, furious at having their plans defeated, for they intended me to marry the king of the dwarfs and I utterly refused, changed me into a white cat. When they brought me here I found all the lords and ladies of my father's court awaiting me under the same enchantment, with the people of lesser rank invisible, all but their hands.

"As they laid me under the enchantment, the fairies told me all my history, for until then I had quite believed that I was their child. But they warned me that my only chance of regaining my natural form was to win the love of a prince who resembled in every way my unfortunate lover."

"And you have won it, lovely princess," interrupted the prince.

"You are indeed wonderfully like him," resumed the princess—"in voice, in features, and everything. And if you really love me my troubles will be at an end."

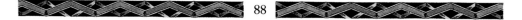

"And mine too," cried the prince, throwing himself at her feet, "if you will consent to marry me."

"I love you already better than anyone in the world," she said. "But now it is time to go back to your father, and we shall hear what he says about it."

So the prince gave her his hand and led her out, and they mounted the chariot together. It was even more splendid than before, and so was the whole company. Even the horses' shoes were of rubies with diamond nails.

The princess was as kind and clever as she was beautiful, and for the prince it was a delightful journey, for everything the princess said was charming.

When they came near the castle where the brothers were to meet, the princess got into a chair carried by four of the guards. It was hewn of one splendid crystal and had silken curtains, which she drew round her that she might not be seen.

The prince saw his brothers walking upon the terrace, each with a lovely princess. They came to meet him asking if he had also found a

wife. He said that he had found something much rarer—a little white cat! They laughed very much and asked him if he was afraid of being eaten up by mice in the palace. And then they set out together for the town. Each prince and princess rode in a splendid carriage. The horses were decked with plumes of feathers and glittered with gold. After them came the youngest prince, and last of all the crystal chair, at which everybody looked with admiration and curiosity. When the courtiers saw them coming they hastened to tell the king.

"Are the ladies beautiful?" he asked anxiously.

And when they answered that nobody had ever before seen such lovely princesses the king seemed quite annoyed. He received them graciously, however, but found it impossible to choose between them.

Then turning to his youngest son he said, "Have you come back alone, after all?"

"Your Majesty," replied the prince, "will find in that crystal chair a little white cat, which has such soft paws and mews so prettily that I am sure you will be charmed with it."

The king smiled and went to draw back the curtains himself, but at a touch from the princess the crystal shivered into a thousand splinters, and there she stood in all her beauty. Her fair hair floated over her shoulders and was crowned with flowers, and her softly falling robe was of the purest white. She saluted the king gracefully, while a murmur of admiration rose from all around.

"Sire," she said, "I have not come to deprive you of the throne you fill so worthily. I have already six kingdoms. Permit me to bestow one upon you and upon each of your sons. I ask nothing but your friendship and your consent to my marriage with your youngest son. We shall still have three kingdoms left for ourselves."

The king and all the courtiers could not conceal their joy and astonishment, and the marriage of the three princes was celebrated at once. The festivities lasted several months, and then each king and queen departed to their own kingdom and lived happily ever after.

Bluebeard

In long ago times, in a splendid house, surrounded by fine gardens and a park, there lived a man who had riches in abundance. He had everything to make him popular except one, and that was his beard. For his beard was neither black as a raven's wing, golden as the sunlight, nor just an ordinary everyday color. It was blue, bright blue. In spite of his blue beard, however, this man had married several times, though what had become of his wives nobody could say.

Not far from Bluebeard's house there lived a widow with two very lovely daughters and one of these Bluebeard wished to marry. Which one he did not care. They could decide between themselves.

Neither of these girls had the least desire to have a husband with a blue beard, and also, not knowing the fate of the other wives, they did not like to risk disappearing from the world as those had done. But being very polite young women they would not refuse Bluebeard's proposals outright.

The younger said, "I would not for a moment take away Sister Anne's chance of marrying such a wealthy man." And Sister Anne declared that, although the elder, she would much prefer to give way to her sister. And so it went on for some time.

Then Bluebeard invited the widow and her daughters to spend a week with him. He also invited many of their neighbors.

Most sumptuous was the entertainment provided for them. Hunting and fishing expeditions, picnics and balls went on from morning till night, and all the night through, so that there was not time even to think of sleep, only feasting and pleasure the whole week long.

So well, indeed, did the younger sister enjoy this, that by the end of the week she had begun to think perhaps after all her host's beard was not so very blue, and that it would be a fine thing to be the mistress of such a magnificent mansion, and the wife of such a rich man.

And so, not long afterward, there was a grand wedding, and the widow's younger daughter became Mrs. Bluebeard.

About a month later, Bluebeard told his wife that he must leave her for several weeks, having to travel on business.

"While I am absent, my dear," said he, "invite your relatives and friends and enjoy yourself just as you please in entertaining them. Here are my keys, the keys to the rooms and to the chests where I keep my money, my gold and silver, and my jewels. Unlock rooms and chests and use freely what you will.

"This small key," he added, pointing to quite a little one, "is the key to the door at the end of the lower landing. You will not need to use this at all. In fact, should you open that door, or even put this key into the lock, I will be dreadfully angry; indeed, I will make you suffer for it in a terrible way."

Then Bluebeard bid his wife goodbye, and departed.

As soon as Mrs. Bluebeard's friends and relations knew that her husband was away, they came flocking to visit her, for they longed to see all her splendid possessions, but had feared to come before.

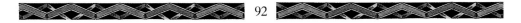

They could not admire enough the magnificent apartments, and ran from one to another praising everything they saw.

But the young wife heeded nothing they said or did. All she thought of was that little key which she must not use, wondering more and more why she ought not to open that one particular door.

At last she could bear it no longer. Slipping away from her visitors, she ran along the passages and stairs, nearly falling down them, so great was her haste, until she came to that door at the end of the corridor.

Not pausing an instant, she thrust the key into the lock, and the door sprang open.

At first she could distinguish nothing, for the room was dark and gloomy. But then, all of a sudden, she knew what had become of Bluebeard's other wives, for there they lay, in a long, straight row, all dead. She stood horrified for a moment or two, gazing at the pale faces, and long hair spread out around them. Then picking up the little key, which she had taken from the lock but dropped in her fright, she hastily left the room, shut and locked the door, and ran to her own chamber to calm herself before returning to her guests. But she was unable to rest for an instant, so dreadful were her feelings. Then with terror she noticed that on the key there was a stain. She wiped it with her handkerchief, but alas! it was blood that would not be wiped away. She washed the key and rubbed it, and scraped it and polished it, but all to no purpose. If she succeeded in cleansing one side, the mark came out on the other. For the key was enchanted.

That same evening Bluebeard returned saying he had met the man whom he had wanted to see, and so the long journey was unnecessary, and he was happy to be at home again.

Next morning he asked for the keys. His wife brought them to him, but not the little one. That one she left behind. Bluebeard noticed this immediately and sent her to fetch it. Trembling, and white as a sheet, she was forced to give it to him.

"Ha! What is this?" he cried. "What is this stain that I see!"

His poor wife trembled still more, and could not speak.

"Wretched woman!" shouted Bluebeard. "You have used this key. You have unlocked the door of that room at the end of the passage. You shall die!"

His wife pleaded with him to spare her, kneeling before him with tears streaming from her eyes.

"You shall die!" he cried again, more savagely than before.

"Let me have a few moments alone, to prepare for death."

"Half a quarter of an hour, but not a moment longer," he replied, and left her.

The poor young woman hastened to a room at the foot of the turret stairs where her sister Anne was.

"Sister Anne, Sister Anne," she called. "Look from the tower window. Can you see anyone coming?"

And Sister Anne, looking out, answered, "Alas! No! Nothing but the green grass, and the sun which shines upon it."

Bluebeard shouted from below that the time was almost up.

"Sister Anne, Sister Anne, look once again, can you see anyone coming?" whispered the young wife wringing her hands. Her brothers, she knew, were to visit her that day. If only they would come in time!

"Alas, no!" Sister Anne replied. "I see a cloud of dust, but it is only a flock of sheep on the road."

Now Bluebeard bawled out so loudly for his wife to come down, that the whole house shook.

"Sister Anne, Sister Anne, tell me is anyone coming?"

"I see two horsemen afar off," cried Sister Anne. "I will beckon to them so they will hurry."

But Bluebeard would wait not a moment longer. Nearly dead with terror his wife descended, still entreating him to spare her life.

He would not, however, listen to her. He was just brandishing his sword, so that it might come down straight and true upon her slender neck, when the door burst open. Two young army officers came rushing in, whom Bluebeard recognized as the brothers of his wife. He swiftly fled, but they speedily followed, and for his many crimes they slew him then and there.

All his wealth now belonged to his widow, and she gratefully rewarded her brothers by purchasing them commissions in the army. She settled a large sum of money upon her sister, and after a while she married again, and with a good husband lived a happy life.

Tufty Riquet

Once upon a time there was a queen who had the ugliest little baby imaginable, so ugly indeed, that it was almost impossible to believe he was a little boy at all.

A fairy, however, assured his mother that the little baby would be very good and clever, saying that she was also giving him a gift which would enable him to make the person whom he loved the best as clever as himself.

This somewhat consoled the queen, but still she was very unhappy because her son was so ugly. No sooner had the boy begun to speak than he could talk about all sorts of things, and he had such pretty ways that people were charmed with him.

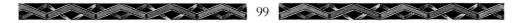

I forgot to say that, when he was quite a baby, he had a funny little tuft of hair on his head, so he was called Tufty Riquet, for Riquet was the family name.

When Riquet was about seven years old, the queen of a kingdom nearby had two baby daughters, twins, of whom one was so exquisitely beautiful that the queen nearly died of joy when she saw her, and so the fairy, the same one who had given Riquet his gift of cleverness, to keep the queen from making herself ill with excitement, told her that this little princess would not be at all clever, indeed she would be as stupid as she was beautiful.

The queen was very much grieved at this, and felt still more troubled when she beheld her other daughter, for the second princess was extremely ugly.

"Do not take it too much to heart, madam," remarked the fairy, "for this second daughter will be so clever that it will scarcely be noticed that she is not beautiful."

"Well, if it must be so, it must," remarked the queen, "but I should certainly have liked the elder one, who is beautiful, to be just a little bit clever too."

"I can do nothing about her mind, madam," replied the fairy, "but for her beauty I can, and since there is nothing I would not do to please you, I will give her a gift so that she can make the one who wins her heart beautiful too."

As the princesses grew up, their gifts grew with them, so that everybody spoke about the beauty of the one and the cleverness of the other. But their defects also grew, so that it could not but be noticed that the younger was daily uglier, and the elder day by day became more stupid, until she either said nothing in reply to a question, or said something quite silly. And she was so clumsy that she could not arrange four china ornaments on the mantelpiece without breaking one, or drink a glass of water without spilling half of it on her frock.

Although it is a nice thing to have beauty, the younger sister generally

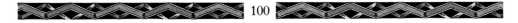

received more attention in company than her elder sister. At first, everybody would gather around the beautiful one admiringly, but before long they would leave her for the clever princess, to listen to her pleasant conversation. And by the end of a quarter of an hour the elder would be left alone, while the other would be the center of a group.

This the elder sister noticed, in spite of her stupidity, and she would gladly have given all her beauty for half the cleverness of her sister. Sometimes the queen, although full of kindness, would reproach her daughter for her foolishness, which caused the princess almost to die of grief.

One day when she had retreated to a wood to brood over her unhappiness, she saw a little man coming toward her. He was uncommonly ugly and unpleasing in appearance, but was very richly dressed.

It was the young Prince Tufty Riquet, who had fallen in love with the pictures he had seen of the beautiful princess, and had left his father's kingdom for the sake of making her acquaintance.

Delighted to meet her alone in this manner, he accosted her as courteously as possible, but soon, noticing that she was melancholy, he said, "I cannot understand how it is that anyone as beautiful as you are can be as sad as you appear to be. I must admit, that although I can boast of having seen many beauties, not one have I ever met whose beauty equalled yours."

"It pleases you to say so, sir," replied the princess, and relapsed into silence.

"Beauty," went on Riquet, "is so delightful that one would give everything for it, and if anyone is beautiful I can't understand anything troubling greatly."

"I would rather be as ugly as you," answered the princess, "and be clever, than as beautiful as I am, and be stupid."

"To think you are stupid is a sure sign that you have a certain amount of cleverness, madam," replied Riquet.

"I don't think about that," said the princess, "but I am quite sure that

I am very silly, and the grief of that is making me very unhappy."

"If that is all that troubles you, I can soon put an end to your grief," said Riquet, "for I have the power of giving cleverness to the person whom I love the best, and if you will marry me, you shall become as clever as you can wish."

103

The princess was greatly astonished, but remained silent.

"I can see," continued Riquet, "that this proposal is not to your taste, and I am not astonished. I will give you a year to think about it."

So great was the longing of the princess to be clever, that she at once promised Riquet to marry him in a year's time. No sooner had she made the promise than a great change took place in her, and she found she could say all sorts of pleasant things, on all sorts of subjects, in quite an easy manner.

She at once began a conversation with Riquet, making such brilliant remarks, that he could almost think he had given her all his cleverness and had kept none for himself.

When the princess returned to the palace, everybody was astonished at the sudden and extraordinary change, for, instead of saying stupid things, or just nothing at all, she was now full of beautiful ideas which she expressed most charmingly.

The report of this transformation was soon spread abroad, and all the young princes of the neighboring kingdoms asked for her hand in marriage. But not one did she find altogether suitable.

At last one arrived, however, who was so powerful, rich, clever and handsome that she could not help approving of him, and her father, noticing this, told her she was quite free to choose the husband she wished.

The princess thanked him, and asked for time to consider the matter.

Then, to think it over, she went by chance into the wood where she had met Tufty Riquet.

While she was walking, deep in thought, she noticed a loud noise beneath her feet, as of many persons hastening to and fro. Listening attentively, she heard a voice say, "Bring me the saucepan," and another voice cry, "Put some wood on the fire."

At the same moment the earth opened and she saw a big kitchen full of cooks, all sorts of things necessary for the making of a magnificent banquet, and everybody hard at work.

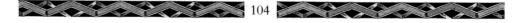

The princess, astonished at this sight, asked the men for whom they were working.

"For the Prince Tufty Riquet," answered the head cook. "Tomorrow is his wedding day."

The princess, more surprised than ever, all at once recollected that it was just a year ago that very day that she had promised to marry the ugly Tufty Riquet.

The reason that she had not remembered her promise before was that she was foolish when she made it, and in becoming clever she had forgotten all her former stupidities.

She had only walked a few steps further, when Riquet appeared before her, magnificently clad, as a prince about to marry.

"Here you see me, madam," said he, "keeping my word, and I have no doubt that you also came here to keep yours, and by giving me your hand to make me the happiest of men."

"I frankly confess," replied the princess, "that I have not yet made up my mind, and I do not think I can ever do as you wish."

"You surprise me, madam," said Riquet.

"I can quite believe that," said the princess, "and if you were not a good and clever man, I should not know how to act. But you are well aware that it was when I was stupid that I promised to marry you, but now, as you may imagine, I am not so easily pleased."

"Except for my ugliness," said Riquet, "have you anything against me? Do you object to my birth, my character, or my manners?"

"Not at all," replied the princess. "I love those things in you."

"If that is so," answered Riquet, "I shall indeed be made happy, because you can cause me to become the most delightful of men if only you will desire it. For know, madam, the same fairy who at my birth gave me the power to impart cleverness to whomsoever I should love, gave you a gift also, that of being able to render beautiful the one to whom you would grant this favor."

"If that is the case," exclaimed the princess, "I desire with all my heart that you might be the most handsome and pleasing prince in the world."

No sooner had the princess uttered these words than her wish was fulfilled, though some say that no change really took place in Riquet, but that the princess now loved him so much that all his ugliness was seen as beauty by her eyes.

However that may be, she immediately consented to be his bride, and, as the preparations had already been made, the wedding took place the very next day.

Hansel and Gretel

Once upon a time there dwelt on the outskirts of a large forest a poor woodcutter with his wife and two children. The boy was called Hansel and the girl Gretel. The woodcutter had always little enough to live on, and once, when there was a great famine, he could not even provide his children with daily bread.

One night, as he was tossing about in bed, full of cares and worry, he sighed and said to his wife, who was the children's stepmother, "What's to become of us? How are we to support our poor children, now that we have nothing more for ourselves?"

"I'll tell you what, husband," answered the woman. "Early tomorrow morning we'll take the children out into the thickest part of the wood. There we shall light a fire for them and give them each a piece of bread. Then we'll go on to our work and leave them alone. They won't be able to find their way home, and we shall thus be rid of them."

"No, wife," said the woodcutter, "that I won't do. How could I find

it in my heart to leave my children alone in the wood? The wild beasts would soon come and tear them to pieces."

"Oh! You fool," said she, "then we must all four die of hunger, and you may just as well go and plane the boards for our coffins." And she left him no peace until he consented.

"But I can't help feeling sorry for the poor children," added the husband.

The children, too, had not been able to sleep for hunger, and had heard what their stepmother had said to their father. Gretel wept bitterly and said to Hansel, "Now it's all up with us."

"No, no, Gretel," said Hansel, "don't worry. I'll be able to find a way of escape, no fear."

And when the old people had fallen asleep he got up, slipped on his little coat, opened the back door, and stole out. The moon was shining clearly, and the white pebbles which lay in front of the house glittered like bits of silver. Hansel bent down and filled his pocket with as many of them as he could cram in. Then he went back and said to Gretel, "Be comforted, my dear little sister, and go to sleep. God will not desert us," and he lay down in bed again.

At daybreak, even before the sun was up, the woman came and woke the two children. "Get up, you lie-abeds, we're all going to the forest to fetch wood." She gave them each a bit of bread. "Here's something for your luncheon, but don't you eat it up before, for it's all you'll get."

Gretel put the bread under her apron, since Hansel had the stones in his pocket. Then they all set out together on the way to the forest.

After they had walked for a little, Hansel stood still and looked back at the house. He repeated this maneuver again and again.

His father observed him and said, "Hansel, what are you gazing at there, and why do you always remain behind? Take care, and don't lose your footing."

"Oh! Father," said Hansel, "I am looking back at my white kitten, which is sitting on the roof, waving me a farewell."

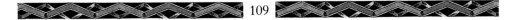

The woman exclaimed, "What a donkey you are! That isn't your kitten. That's the morning sun shining on the chimney." But Hansel had not looked back at his kitten. He had always dropped one of the white pebbles out of his pocket onto the path.

When they had reached the middle of the forest the father said, "Now, children, go and fetch a lot of wood, and I'll light a fire so that you won't feel cold."

Hansel and Gretel heaped up brushwood until they had made a pile nearly the size of a small hill. The brushwood was set fire to, and when the flames leaped high the woman said, "Now lie down at the fire, children, and rest yourselves. We are going into the forest to cut down wood. When we've finished we'll come back and fetch you."

Hansel and Gretel sat down beside the fire. At midday they ate their little bits of bread. They heard the strokes of the ax, so they thought their father was quite near. But it was no ax they heard. It was a bough he had tied onto a dead tree, and that was blown about by the wind. And when they had sat for a long time their eyes closed with fatigue, and they fell fast asleep.

When they awoke at last it was pitch dark. Gretel began to cry and said, "How are we ever to get out of the wood?"

Hansel comforted her. "Wait a bit," he said, "until the moon is up, and then we'll find our way sure enough."

And when the full moon had risen Hansel took his sister by the hand and followed the pebbles, which shone like new threepenny bits and showed them the path. They walked all through the night. At daybreak they reached their father's house again. They knocked at the door, and when the woman opened it she exclaimed, "You naughty children, what a time you've slept in the wood! We thought you were never going to come back."

The father rejoiced, for his conscience had reproached him for leaving his children behind by themselves.

Not long afterward there was again great dearth in the land, and the

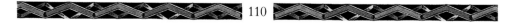

children heard their stepmother say to their father in bed one night, "Everything is eaten up once more. We have only half a loaf in the house, and when that's finished it's all up with us. The children must be got rid of. We'll lead them deeper into the wood this time, so that they won't be able to find their way out again. There is no other way of saving ourselves."

The man's heart smote him heavily, and he thought, Surely it would be better to share the last bite with one's children! But his wife wouldn't listen to his arguments, and did nothing but scold and reproach him. If a

man yields once he's done for, and so, because he had given in the first time, he was forced to do so the second.

But the children were awake and had heard the conversation. When the old people were asleep Hansel got up and wanted to go out and pick up pebbles again, as he had done the first time. But the woman had barred the door and Hansel couldn't get out. But he consoled his little sister and said, "Don't cry, Gretel, and sleep peacefully, for God is sure to help us."

At early dawn the woman came and made the children get up. They received their bit of bread, but it was even smaller than the time before. On the way to the wood Hansel crumbled it in his pocket, and every few minutes he stood still and dropped a crumb on the ground.

"Hansel, what are you stopping and looking about you for?" said the father.

"I'm looking back at my little pigeon, which is sitting on the roof waving me a farewell," answered Hansel.

"Fool!" said the wife. "That isn't your pigeon, it's the morning sun glittering on the chimney."

But Hansel gradually threw all his crumbs onto the path.

The woman led the children still deeper into the forest, further than they had ever been in their lives before. Then a big fire was lit again, and the stepmother said, "Just sit down there, children, and if you're tired you can sleep a bit. We're going into the forest to cut down wood, and in the evening when we're finished we'll come back to fetch you."

At midday Gretel divided her bread with Hansel, for he had strewn his all along their path. Then they fell asleep, and evening passed, but nobody came to the poor children.

They didn't awake until it was pitch dark, and Hansel comforted his sister, saying, "Only wait, Gretel, until the moon rises, then we shall see the bread crumbs I scattered along the path. They will show us the way back to the house."

When the moon appeared they got up, but they found no crumbs, for the thousands of birds that fly about the woods and fields had picked

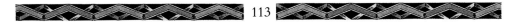

them all up. "Never mind," said Hansel to Gretel, "you'll see we'll still find a way out." But all the same they did not. They wandered about the whole night, and the next day, from morning until evening, but they could not find a path out of the wood. They were very hungry, too, for they had nothing to eat but a few berries they found on the ground. And at last they were so tired that their legs refused to carry them any longer, so they lay down under a tree and fell fast asleep.

On the third morning after they had left their father's house they set about their wandering again, but only got deeper and deeper into the wood. Now they felt that if help did not come to them soon they must perish.

At midday they saw a beautiful little snow-white bird sitting on a branch. The bird sang so sweetly that they stopped and listened to it. And when its song was finished it flapped its wings and flew on in front of them. They followed it and came to a little house, on the roof of which it perched. When they came quite near they saw that the cottage was made of bread and roofed with cakes, while the window was made of transparent sugar.

"Now we'll have plenty to eat," said Hansel. "I'll eat a bit of the roof, and you, Gretel, can eat some of the window, which you'll find deliciously sweet." Hansel stretched up his hand and broke off a little bit of the roof to see what it was like, and Gretel went to the casement and began to nibble at it. Thereupon a shrill voice called out from the room inside:

"Nibble, nibble, little mouse,
Who's nibbling my house?"

The children answered,

"'Tis heaven's own child,
The tempest wild,"

and continued to eat without thinking about the voice. Hansel, who thoroughly appreciated the roof, tore down a big bit of it, while Gretel pushed out a whole round windowpane, and sat down the better to enjoy it.

Suddenly the door opened and an ancient woman leaning on a staff hobbled out. Hansel and Gretel were so terrified that they let what they had in their hands fall.

But the old woman shook her head and said, "Oh, ho! you dear children, who led you here? Just come in and stay with me. No ill shall befall you." She took them each by the hand and led them into the house, and laid a most sumptuous dinner before them—milk and sugared pancakes, with apples and nuts. After they had finished, two beautiful little white beds were prepared for them. When Hansel and Gretel lay down in them they felt as if they had got into heaven.

The old woman had appeared to be most friendly, but she was really an old witch who had waylaid the children, and had only built the little gingerbread house to lure them in. When anyone came into her power she killed, cooked, and ate him, and held a regular feast day for the occasion. Now, witches have red eyes and cannot see far, but, like beasts, they have a keen sense of smell and know when human beings pass by. When

Hansel and Gretel fell into her hands she laughed maliciously and said to herself: "I've got them now; they shan't escape me."

Early in the morning, before the children were awake, she arose, and when she saw them both sleeping so peacefully, with their round rosy cheeks, she muttered to herself, "That'll be a dainty bite." Then she seized Hansel with her bony hand, carried him into a little stable, and barred the door on him. He might scream as much as he liked, it did him no good. Then she went to Gretel, shook her until she awoke, and cried, "Get up, you lazybones. Fetch water and cook something for your brother. When he's fat I'll eat him up." Gretel began to cry bitterly, but it was of no use: she had to do what the wicked witch bade her.

So the best food was cooked for poor Hansel, but Gretel got nothing but crab shells. Every morning the old woman hobbled out to the stable

and cried, "Hansel, put out your finger, that I may feel if you are getting fat." But Hansel always stretched out a bone, and the old dame, whose eyes were dim, couldn't see it, and thinking always it was Hansel's finger, wondered why he fattened so slowly.

When four weeks passed and Hansel still remained thin, she lost patience and decided to wait no longer. "Hi! Gretel," she called to the girl, "be quick and get some water. Hansel may be fat or thin, I'm going to kill him tomorrow and cook him."

Oh! how the poor little sister sobbed as she carried the water, and how the tears rolled down her cheeks! "Kind heaven help us now!" she cried. "If only the wild beasts in the wood had eaten us, then at least we should have died together."

"Just hold your peace," said the old hag. "It won't help you."

Early in the morning Gretel had to go out and hang up the kettle full of water and light the fire. "First we'll bake," said the old dame. "I've heated the oven already and kneaded the dough." She pushed Gretel out to the oven, from which fiery flames were already issuing. "Creep in," said the witch, "and see if it's properly heated, so that we can shove in the bread." For when she had got Gretel in she meant to close the oven and let the girl bake, that she might eat her up too.

But Gretel perceived her intention and said, "I don't know how I'm to do it. How do I get in?"

"You silly goose!" said the hag, "the opening is big enough. See, I could get in myself." And she crawled toward it and poked her head into the oven. Then Gretel gave her a shove that sent her right in, shut the iron door, and drew the bolt. Gracious! How she yelled! It was quite horrible. But Gretel fled, and the wretched old witch was left to perish miserably.

Gretel flew straight to Hansel, opened the little stable door, and cried, "Hansel, we are free. The old witch is dead." Then Hansel sprang like a bird out of a cage when the door is opened.

How they rejoiced, and fell on each other's necks, and jumped for joy, and kissed one another! And since they no longer had any cause for fear,

they went into the old hag's house. There they found, in every corner of the room, boxes with pearls and precious stones.

"These are even better than pebbles," said Hansel, and crammed his pockets full of them. And Gretel said, "I too will bring something home" and she filled her apron full.

"But now," said Hansel, "let's go and get well away from the witch's wood." When they had wandered about for some hours they came to a big lake.

"We can't get over," said Hansel. "I see no bridge of any sort or kind."

"Yes, and there's no ferryboat either," answered Gretel. "But look, there's a white duck. If I ask her she'll help us over." She called out:

> "Here are two children, mournful very,
> Seeing neither bridge nor ferry;
> Take us upon your white back,
> And row us over quack, quack!"

The duck swam toward them, and Hansel got on her back and bade his little sister sit beside him. "No," answered Gretel, "we should be too heavy a load for the duck. She shall carry us across separately."

The good bird did this, and when they were both landed safely on the other side and had gone on for a while the wood became more and more familiar to them. Finally, they saw their father's house in the distance. Then they set off to run, and bounding into the room they fell on their father's neck. Their father had not passed a happy hour since he left them in the wood, but his wife had died.

Gretel shook out her apron so that the pearls and precious stones rolled about the room, and Hansel threw down one handful after the other out of his pocket. Thus all their troubles were ended, and they all lived happily ever afterward.